knew it almost as intimately as she knew her own. Even from across the room, Dallas's hands could feel its contours, and her own body knew the way it would fit against her.

Get hold of yourself. You've never seen this man before.

"Dorthea McAllister?" the stranger said uncertainly. "What is this place? Where are we?"

"How do you know my name?" It wasn't quite her name, but it was too close to be accidental.

The stranger who'd seemed to materialize in her office offered no explanation. Dallas came out from behind her desk and slowly approached him. He didn't appear dangerous, only disoriented, and somehow intriguing. A faded flannel shirt hung in shreds around his midsection, revealing a lean, sinewy body.

"This is the Los Reales City Hall," she told him. "Is there anything I can do to help you, Mr...." She paused, hoping he would fill in his name.

His bewildered expression grew stronger. "Don't you know me, Dorthea?"

"No."

"But I am Miguel! *Querida mia,* surely you haven't forgotten. Today is Christmas Eve. Tomorrow is our wedding day!"

Dear Reader,

You're about to step under the mistletoe with one of our four hunky heroes this month in our CHRISTMAS KISSES holiday promotion!

For Patricia Chandler, Christmas in the Southwest, which she calls home, is special. The Mission San Xavier del Bac she writes about, also known as the White Dove of the Desert, has witnessed generations of Christmas worshipers. Poinsettia trees bloom, locals decorate the traditional Spanish town squares with thousands of lights and children celebrate *posadas*, recreating Mary and Joseph's first night in Bethlehem.

Pat and all of us at Harlequin wish you a joyous holiday filled with CHRISTMAS KISSES!

Debra Matteucci
Senior Editor and Editorial Coordinator
Harlequin Books
300 E. 42nd St.
New York, NY 10017

PATRICIA CHANDLER

A TIMELESS CHRISTMAS

Harlequin Books

TORONTO • NEW YORK • LONDON
AMSTERDAM • PARIS • SYDNEY • HAMBURG
STOCKHOLM • ATHENS • TOKYO • MILAN
MADRID • WARSAW • BUDAPEST • AUCKLAND

ISBN 0-373-16564-1

A TIMELESS CHRISTMAS

Chapter One

Across the desert floor slick with snow, Miguel de Pima ran for his life.

He lost his footing on a small incline and fell, rolling over and over until he crashed into a cholla cactus as big as a man. Its vicious clawed spines pierced the cloth of his shirtsleeve and caught like a thousand tiny fishhooks the flesh beneath it.

Mindless of the pain that seared through him as the spines shredded his flesh, Miguel tore himself away from the cholla, and scrambled to his feet and pushed on, not losing a beat in the rhythm of his desperate flight.

He risked a quick glance over his shoulder. His pursuers were nowhere in sight, but he knew they were not far behind. He knew they would have no trouble following him. The snow guaranteed it.

Madre de Dios, never could he remember such a snowfall! Every winter brought a layer of snow to the high mountains that circled Tucson Valley and occasionally a light dusting to the desert floor, as well.

But *this!*

This snow lay nearly as high as the tops of his boots, and still it continued to fall. It crushed the fragile vegetation and hid the many small, subtle landmarks that a man needed as guideposts through the desert, giving the normally familiar terrain an eerie, unearthly quality, and making it difficult for even an experienced tracker like himself to find his way.

The Mission! Miguel thought desperately. If he could just make it to the Mission! Father Sebastiani, unwilling though he was to involve himself with politics, would surely not refuse to help him!

And there Dorthea would be waiting. As long as they were together, he knew all would be well. *Dorthea.*

Dreamlike, her face floated uncertainly before his exhausted eyes. Her flame-colored hair was the only bright spot in the otherwise dismal landscape, and it seemed to him a beacon, showing him the way he must go.

He had been running so long in the bitter cold that his mind, as well as his body, was numb. No longer sure what was real and what was not, he followed Dorthea's flaming hair like a candle in the night.

And it didn't fail him. Suddenly before him stood the Mission San Xavier del Bac, gleaming whitely under the pale moon. It was as blurred and indistinct as the vision of Dorthea's beloved face, and for an instant Miguel doubted its reality. He blinked to clear his vision, and Dorthea's face disappeared, but the Mission did not.

Risking another glance backward, he saw that his own footsteps blazed an unmistakable trail in the snow, and beside them, a steady stream of dark drops that was his own blood. The men who pursued him were still out of sight, but he could hear the thunder of their horses' hooves—they sounded as loud as his own thundering heart. He could almost feel the horses' cold breath on the back of his neck.

Crouched low to the ground, he put on a burst of speed that carried him to the white adobe walls of Mission San Xavier del Bac, and threw himself with a bone-crunching thud against the portal's heavy mesquite door.

FATHER SEBASTIANI took his place at the back of the church and waited for the children to arrive. Already he could hear their high, sweet voices singing as their *Las Posadas* procession came nearer.

It was Christmas Eve, the last night of Advent. Every evening since December 13th, the Indian children from the Mission's school formed *Las Posadas*—a procession that reenacted the first Christmas when Mary and Joseph journeyed on a donkey to Bethlehem and found no room at the inn.

For the past eleven nights, their procession had visited homes in the Indian village of Tubac, where they had been first turned away, then invited inside for sweets and games as was the tradition. But on this night, on Christmas Eve, the procession would come to the church, where the child representing Mary would place the doll she carried in the straw-filled manger below the altar steps.

Father Sebastiani folded his hands across his ample belly and tried to let the beauty of the ritual and the peace of the season overtake him.

But he could not.

There was trouble in the town of Los Reales. Not a town, really, the friar corrected himself. Huddled against the thick walls of the presidio, some five miles to the west, Los Reales was no more than a collection of rough shelters clinging to the fort's adobe walls for protection from the Apaches.

But town or not, it had more than its share of trouble this night. And it had nothing to do with the Apaches.

The frightened but determined young woman hidden at this very moment in Father Sebastiani's sacristy had brought him the news. Now he waited in sorrow for Miguel de Pima, the brightest pupil who had ever attended his school, and the one for whom Father Sebastiani had had the highest hopes. And he waited also for the men he knew would follow.

His heart prayed for the follies of men, and that the violence that was surely coming would wait until after the children had completed their Christmas celebration.

Upon hearing a loud and unexpected thud against the heavy portal of his church, Father Sebastiani understood that God had not seen fit to grant his prayer.

"BEGGIN' YER PARDON, Farrtherrr, we come fer the lad." The cowboy who spoke for the posse at his back had bright red hair and a Scot's brogue. Obviously, a McAllister, and obviously a recent immigrant, since the rolling of his r's was quite thick.

Damn Red McAllister, Father Sebastiani growled to himself, not even bothering to ask God to forgive him the sin of blasphemy. *He'll soon have the entire valley overrun with his kin.*

"Welcome to the House of the Lord on this holiest of nights," was all he said aloud, in a voice that sounded almost as though he meant it. "You have come to join our procession?"

The redheaded cowboy looked uncomfortable. "We come fer the lad...." he began again, haltingly.

Father Sebastiani considered denying that Miguel was there, but immediately thought better of it. Not even he had missed the footprints in the snow. "What business do you have with him?" he temporized.

"He's a thief," snarled another angry voice. "We're gonna hang 'im."

The horses were restive, sensing the tension in the air. Suddenly several whinnied and sidestepped skittishly as from their midst a magnificent stallion pranced forward.

The stallion stood at least seventeen hands, so black as to appear no more than a blacker shadow in the black of the night. The man who sat astride him, dressed in black, seemed also no more than a shadow, except for the pale oval of his face gashed by a cruel sneer of a mouth.

The stallion reared, its hooves hovering dangerously above Father Sebastiani's squat form. "We want the Indian, Priest," the dark rider spat contemptuously.

Father Sebastiani again recognized the Scot's brogue. He recognized the arrogant authority in the voice. It was Judge Red McAllister himself. Many in the territory, some out of admiration, some out of loathing, called him "The Hangin' Judge"; to his face, most simply referred to him as "The McAllister."

Father Sebastiani's voice assumed the even greater authority of his own office. "He has sought sanctuary in God's House," he said with quiet dignity. "You may not take him."

"He's a thief and a fugitive from the law," The McAllister countered, his brogue thick. "I'll have him, all right."

"Miguel de Pima is no thief," Father Sebastiani protested.

"I caught him watering his horse at my well. That makes him a thief."

"The wells belong to everyone, Judge," the priest countered bravely. "Who can presume to own the water God has provided for His children in this scorched land?''

''*I* can, Priest. The water belongs to whomever is strong enough to take it.'' The stallion reared again, grazing Father Sebastiani's brown cassock menacingly as its rider urged it through the open portal and into the candlelit interior of the church. Several riders followed, and the clatter of horses' hooves on the clay tiles echoed through the high-domed ceilings.

Father Sebastiani hurried to head off the intruders, then turned to confront them. ''He has taken sanctuary in God's House,'' he cried, spreading his arms wide as if to block their way. ''This is sacrilege! You may not do this thing!''

The McAllister advanced his stallion farther, and the friar found himself forced to retreat. His arms still outspread, demanding that the posse desist, he backed toward the altar, where stood Miguel de Pima.

''Place yourself under the protection of the Cross!'' he shouted to Miguel. ''Not even these heathen will dare desecrate the sanctity of the altar!''

The terrified young Indian clung to the feet of the Christ that hung on the cross above the altar. The McAllister squeezed his knees just the slightest bit, and the huge stallion jumped the barrier of the communion rail as delicately as if it were not even there at all.

Advancing on Miguel, The McAllister raised the whip he held in his hand. With a contemptuous flick of his wrist, he slashed away what was left of Miguel's bloody shirt. Then he slashed again, wrapping the tip of the whip around Miguel's hands. The pain forced him to release the crucifix.

"*No, Papa!*"

From the sacristy appeared the young woman who had been waiting there all evening for Miguel. She ran to where he lay beneath the crucifix and dropped to the floor beside him, taking his bloodied head into her lap.

Father Sebastiani groaned. The shawl the girl had been wearing slipped from her head, revealing to him for the first time her thick, curling hair. Her flaming red hair.

Her McAllister hair.

He groaned again. Now he knew Miguel was doomed.

At a curt jerk of The McAllister's head, a cowboy rode up from the rear, leading a riderless horse. Dismounting, he tried to separate the Indian and the redheaded McAllister woman, but she flew at him like a banshee, all claws and teeth and wild, well-aimed limbs.

Quickly a second man came to the aid of the first. He dragged the hysterical girl away and held her tightly—but respectfully, seeing as how she was, after all, The McAllister's daughter—while the first one tied the Indian's hands behind his back, then boosted him roughly onto the spare horse.

The posse turned to go. The clatter of horses' hooves on the tiles and the spine-chilling screams of The McAllister's daughter, Dorthea, echoed together like a demon's chorus through the domes of the high-beamed ceiling.

THE POSSE didn't ride far. Only as far as the nearest mesquite. Mesquite wasn't the best choice for a hanging tree, but this one was old and twisted and tall, and had good, thick branches.

The unnatural snowfall swirled thickly, although there was no wind. It made running difficult. The wet and bedraggled hem of Dorthea's white dress—it was to have been her wedding dress—weighed heavily behind her as she and Father Sebastiani struggled through the snow.

By the time they caught up with the posse, someone had already thrown a rope over a suitable branch and looped the hangman's noose around Miguel's neck.

"You must not do this!" Father Sebastiani demanded. In desperation, he stumbled from one mounted cowboy to another. "You must not murder this innocent man!"

Finally reaching The McAllister's black stallion, Father Sebastiani clutched at the silver-encrusted, Spanish-leather saddle. "You have desecrated God's House and violated His sanctuary!" he cried passionately. "You must not compound these evils with the murder of this innocent man!"

The McAllister looked down at the unprepossessing little priest, his eyes colder than the snow that swirled around them. Then, slowly and deliberately, he raised the rifle that lay across his saddle, pointed it toward the sky, and pulled the trigger.

The snow swirled. Dorthea fell to her knees on the wet ground. The horse beneath Miguel squealed in panic, then bolted. It was found the next day, exhausted and covered with sweat, many miles away from the old mesquite.

By that time Miguel's body had been cut down and buried in the frozen ground.

Chapter Two

Dallas McAllister studied the police report on her desk.

Name: Dennis Joaquin, Jr. Age: 15. Driving without a license. Driving while intoxicated. Destroying public property. Carrying a concealed weapon—a switchblade.

Then she studied the skinny, sullen teenager who stood before her. "Well, Dennis the Menace, I thought I told you the last time you were up before me that I didn't want to see you again. What do you have to say for yourself?"

The boy, wearing on his face the hangdog expression he knew was expected of him, shrugged.

Standing beside him, his father, Dennis Joaquin, Sr., knuckled the side of his son's head with a sharp backhand. "What you say, eh?" he growled.

Dennis the Menace heaved a bored sigh, slouched from one hip to the other, and repeated his shrug.

Dennis, Sr., knuckled his son's head again. "Stupido!" he exclaimed. "Tell the judge why you do these bad things, eh?"

The boy fixed his eyes on two large, framed photographs on the wall behind Dallas's desk. One was the governor of the state of Arizona; the other, one of Dallas's ancestors, the first judge in Los Reales, Judge Red McAllister. He had bushy, frowning eyebrows, a bushy, frowning mustache, and stern, righteous eyes.

Dennis, Dallas guessed, recognized neither.

Shifting his slouch again, he voiced a surly, "Ain't nothin' else to do."

He had a point there, Dallas had to admit.

In Los Reales there were six bars on Main Street alone, and only two churches. There was the old Rialto movie theater that ran feature films ten years out of date, and sold popcorn that tasted even older. There were several video arcades that had offered the same games since they'd opened their doors.

What *was* a teenager to do until he was old enough to spend all of his time and all of his money in the bars with the grown-ups? What *was* there for Dennis the Menace to do until he could become a full-fledged member of the Saturday Night Knife and Gun Club— as she liked to call her group of regulars.

He did what so many of the other kids did—he practiced. He got drunk on beer bought with a fake ID at Larry's Liquor Boutique and ended up joyriding in the desert. Switchblade in his belt, he skulked around the schoolyard the same way he planned to someday skulk around streets and alleys, looking for McAllisters to cut.

And he would find them, or they would find him.

There was, of course, necking behind the tattered screen of the long-closed, drive-in movie. But the druggist at Los Reales's only drugstore refused to sell condoms to anyone under eighteen.

The public health nurse at the high school—an intelligent and farsighted woman, unusual for Los Reales—dispensed them upon request; but no kid worth the name was going to discuss his sex life with a woman who had known him since diaperhood.

Besides, Dallas thought with wry, gallows humor, not even teenagers can make out *all* the time.

She had no answer for Dennis the Menace's sullen observation.

"Dennis," she began sternly, "I can only tell you what I told you the last time. Several of the churches sponsor dances—"

"Kid stuff," he muttered under his breath.

"—and the high school offers after-school activities—"

"Jeez, Judge," Dennis whined as if mortally offended. "I gotta help my old man out, don't I?" His "old man" nodded vigorously. "I ain't got time for no after-school activities."

Sighing, Dallas imposed the same fines she had the last time, forced the boy to listen to the same lecture she had delivered the last time, and released him into the custody of his father, the same as she had the last time.

The same as she would the next time.

Dennis Joaquin, Jr., was the last case on her docket, a docket that had been filled, as the first couple of days of the week always were, with large numbers of shamefaced members of the "Saturday Night Knife and Gun Club."

She glanced at the clock on the wall above the darkening window. It had been a long day, and an exhausting one. It was nearly six o'clock, and the long winter twilight had begun.

Propping her elbows on the desk, Dallas rested her forehead in her hands and gingerly massaged her tired eyes with the heels of her palms.

When she looked up again, there was someone standing at the back of her courtroom.

A man.

One moment the courtroom had been empty, and the next, he was there; and he was motionless, which made it appear that he had been standing there for some time.

Odd, she thought uneasily. She hadn't heard the door push open. She hadn't heard footsteps in the quiet courtroom. And if he had business with the court, why was he standing in the back of the room instead of coming up to her desk?

Suddenly she caught her breath. For a fleeting instant she had the incredible impression that the man standing in the back of her courtroom wasn't quite... *there.* He seemed almost... transparent.

Right through him she could see the miniblinds on the window behind him and the street beyond that, where a tumbleweed as big as a Volkswagen Bug bounced gently down the center white line.

Odder still, he was looking at her almost as though he knew her. And oddest of all, just for a moment Dallas had the uncanny feeling that she knew him, too.

In the next moment she realized that that was impossible. She was acquainted with everyone in town, and this man was most definitely not a stranger...and yet, something buried deep in her subconscious struggled to remember, not *quite* a stranger....

It's been a longer day than I realized, she told herself, staring intently at the man, whose presence appeared to dissolve and then reassemble again.

Then her vision cleared and he became more corporeal. Now he was as substantial as a man should be, which was a relief; now he blocked her view of the street.

His clothes were ragged, and as dusty as the street outside. He must be a ranch hand, she guessed, or maybe a gold prospector down from the hills. *Probably been living in his own company so long he doesn't even realize how disreputable he looks.*

His pants were high-waisted, ill-fitting, almost homemade-looking. His straight black hair was tied away from his face with a red bandanna as ragged as everything else that covered his body.

Around his midsection, a faded flannel shirt hung in shreds. Her eyes were unaccountably drawn to the ragged strips. An involuntary shiver coursed through her. The shredded shirt meant something to her— *what?* Tears welled in the back of her throat—she had no idea why—and she swallowed convulsively, as if trying to hold back a sob.

Beneath the tattered clothes was a lean, sinewy body. A hardworking kind of body, with pick-ax-and-shovel type shoulders. It struck Dallas that she was not only seeing that strong, muscular frame, but *feeling* it, as well.

She *knew* that body, knew it almost as intimately as she knew her own. Even from across the room, her hands could feel its contours, its texture, and her own body knew the way it would fit against hers. Somewhere in the vicinity of her stomach, a secret muscle coiled.

Get hold of yourself, she commanded harshly, but the feeling only grew more intense.

"The office is closed—" she started to say, but her voice came out only an inarticulate whisper. She cleared her throat and began again. "The office is closed now, but if you'll come back tomorrow after 9:00 a.m., someone will be here to help you."

"Dorthea . . . ?" the stranger said uncertainly. He took a hesitant step in Dallas's direction. "What is this place? Where are we?"

Dallas stared at him. "How do you know my name?" Her voice was as uncertain as his had been. It wasn't quite her name, but it was too close to be accidental.

The stranger who was not quite a stranger didn't offer any explanation. He only stood as if rooted to the square foot of cracked linoleum flooring under his feet.

Dallas came out from behind her desk. Carefully, she approached him. "You don't know where you are?" she asked.

A prospector, she decided. *That's what he is. Injured, maybe. Or lost. Sometimes they go a little crazy out there alone in the desert.*

He didn't appear dangerous, though. Only very confused, somewhat disoriented, and somehow intriguing, despite his shabby attire.

"This place is Los Reales City Hall, and we're in my office. I'm afraid we're closed now," she told him for the second time. "But if there's something I can do for you...?"

He looked around the tiny courtroom. "Where is your father?"

"My father?"

"Judge McAllister. Where has he gone?" The man glanced around warily, as though he expected some unseen person to come springing at him from beneath one of the folding chairs.

"There is no Judge McAllister, but I guess I'm what passes for a judge around here. I am Dorothy Alice McAllister, the justice of the peace here in Los Reales."

The stranger focused on the words that were of the most immediate concern to him. "No Judge McAllister?" he repeated. "But you said this *is* Los Reales?"

At Dallas's nod, he looked relieved. "I wasn't sure. Everything seems so changed...."

"It's Los Reales, all right. I don't know how long you've been away, Mr.—Mr...." She paused, waiting for him to fill in his name, but he didn't, so she continued. "But nothing's changed in Los Reales for the twenty-nine years *I've* lived here!"

It was a mild attempt at humor, but it backfired. It took the relief from the stranger's face and left in its place the bewildered, disoriented expression that had been there before.

"You don't know me, Dorthea?" The man looked at her strangely.

The sound of his voice resonated through her. She knew, without questioning *how* she knew it, that she had heard that voice pronounce her name before. For an instant she felt as confused as he.

"No, I don't know you," she finally said. "But tell me your name and maybe it'll come to me."

"But I am *Miguel*...!"

"Miguel...what?"

The stranger looked at her uncomprehendingly. "*Querida mia,* how can you not know my name? I am Miguel. My family is de Pima. How can it be that you have forgotten that?"

"De Pima?" Dallas frowned.

Seldom did de Pimas come over to this side of town. It wasn't safe, even for those wild ones who looked for trouble, who carried knives concealed in their clothing. For *this* particular de Pima, with that dreamy, otherworldly look in his eye, this side of town could be suicide.

"Mr. de Pima," she proposed suddenly, not even sure why she was making the offer at all. "It's getting late. I would be happy to drop you somewhere on my way home. It'd be no problem at all—"

The stranger's attention shifted from Dallas's face to sounds from the street outside.

From a distance, a chorus of high, sweet voices rose and then fell with the rising and falling of the wind.

"It's the children at the elementary school," Dallas explained. "They're having *Las Posadas* celebration."

He looked blank. He didn't appear to be familiar with the beautiful Christmas ritual that had come to the Southwest centuries ago by way of Mexico and the Franciscan friars. Dallas tried to jog his memory.

"You remember *Las Posadas,* don't you?" she prodded gently. "You probably took part in a few of them yourself. It means 'The Inns'? You know, beginning on the thirteenth of December and then every night until Christmas Eve, the children reenact the story of the first Christmas? They go from house to house like Mary and Joseph, trying to find a place to stay for the night?"

She paused. "Do you remember anything like that?"

The man called Miguel didn't seem to be listening. His attention was still fixed on the singing voices in the street. Abruptly he turned back to Dallas.

"*Las Posadas*. Yes, I remember," he replied. "But I thought *Las Posadas* had ended. I heard the children singing, coming into the Mission..." The confusion on his face deepened, then disappeared into a tentative smile. "So it is still Christmas Eve, then? Tomorrow is still our wedding day?"

Dallas stared at him.

"Surely you haven't forgotten, *querida mia?*" He moved a step closer and, before she realized what he had in mind, enfolded her in a firm and intimate embrace. "Tomorrow is our wedding day?"

For the first time since the man had appeared in her courtroom, Dallas was afraid; whether afraid of him or of herself, she wasn't sure. For her reaction to his touch was immediate and instinctive—she melted into his arms as if she belonged there, as if she had waited all her life for just this moment.

In the next instant common sense prevailed. She hadn't felt threatened by his unexpected embrace, she admitted to herself. Rather, she had felt...*cherished.* But all the psychiatric testimony she had listened to over the years echoed through her head. *Delusional. Schizophrenic. Drug-induced psychosis.*

And beyond that, she was a McAllister, and he was a de Pima, and they were alone in a now-deserted area of town where McAllisters and de Pimas had carried on a blood feud for more than one hundred years.

Was he dangerous? Who knew? Maybe he was only...confused. But there was no point in taking any chances. Not with a de Pima. Not in Los Reales.

Envisioning the Winchester 12-gauge leaning against the inside corner of her desk, she disengaged herself from his arms with as much nonchalance as she could muster, then began backing slowly and cautiously across the room.

Don't make any sudden moves, she told herself. *Don't startle him.*

"No," she answered his question in a calm, non-aggressive tone of voice, trying to keep the man's attention on her words and not on the fact that she was imperceptibly putting distance between the two of them.

"It isn't Christmas Eve yet," she continued soothingly. "It's only December thirteenth. It's only the *first* night of *Las Posadas....* "

She gestured in slow motion to the daily calendar that hung between the photographs of the governor of Arizona and the old judge. "See? December thirteenth. The thirteenth of December is the *beginning* of the season. Christmas Eve is the *end...* "

She felt the desk at her back.

Cautiously, not taking her eyes off the stranger, she backed around it and felt with her fingers for the cold steel barrel of the 12-gauge.

She had never had to draw the shotgun, much less fire it. She hated the fact that she felt safer knowing it was there, but there was no denying that she did. Her world, after all, was not a particularly safe place, and self-defense was the foremost thing on any sensible person's mind.

Although she was the law in Los Reales, she was also a McAllister; and the senseless blood feud that had existed between the McAllister and the de Pima factions in town, which had dominated life in Los Reales for nearly a century, occasionally showed an unfortunate tendency to erupt into violence.

Just knowing the 12-gauge was close at hand returned to Dallas a measure of authority. "You'd better go, Mr. de Pima," she suggested coolly. *"Now."*

The man called Miguel looked at Dallas unhappily. "I'm sorry, *querida mia*. I didn't mean to frighten you. The last thing in the world I want to do is cause you any more pain."

"Any...*more* pain?" Dallas whispered unwillingly. Her choice of words seemed an inexplicable response to his statement, she realized vaguely, almost as though they were picking up a conversation interrupted long ago. "When have you ever caused me pain?"

"I am not sure. But I think I must find out." Turning, the stranger headed for the door.

Dallas's first fear was replaced by a new one—the fear that she was going to lose him again. *Again?* She shivered involuntarily. For some reason she couldn't explain, she knew that she didn't want this man, this Miguel de Pima, to disappear from her life as quickly as he had come into it.

"Where will you go?"

"To the Mission, I think. Father Sebastiani will know how to make sense of what is happening to me."

"Let me drive you over," Dallas offered again. Her voice was almost a plea, and this time she didn't even question where the impulse had come from. "It's dark, and it's going to get much colder before long."

Miguel smiled slightly. "No, *querida mia,* your father would miss his wagon. It's better that I do this alone."

"Will I...will I see you again?" Then she reworded the question. "I would like to see you again."

He hesitated. "God willing," he said finally, and then was gone.

Dallas watched him walk beneath a streetlight that briefly illuminated his face, then another, and yet another, until finally he disappeared from view.

Cherished, she thought, feeling his arms around her again. Such a quaint, old-fashioned word. She wondered why it had popped so readily into her head. There were other emotions, too—emotions that shocked her—but they were harder to put into words, and even harder to understand, so Dallas chose not to even try.

MADRE DE DIOS, what had happened to the world since last night? Miguel wondered, his mind in chaos.

What had happened to Dorthea since the last time he had seen her on her knees in the snow?

After all they had been to each other, how could she have forgotten his name?

Miguel had to trust his instincts to guide him, because nothing about Los Reales was familiar, nothing except the fine sand that dusted the hard walkways where wooden boardwalks used to be.

There were many more buildings than he had ever seen, and many appeared to be built of wood, which was generally unavailable in the desert, except to the wealthiest cattlemen, who imported it from the east.

The Cosmopolitan Hotel, the only hotel for miles around, which should have been on the corner in the center of town, was gone.

Everywhere there were flashes of color. Pink and blue and red and white. Looking as though they were somehow lighted from inside, the colors spelled words that Miguel could read, but could make no sense of.

Never could he have imagined such things. He felt as though there were eyes watching him in the dark, and they terrified him.

He heard music and laughter and loud voices that sounded like they came from a bar, but he couldn't see any cluster of horses at a hitching post that would signify Big Lil's or the Last Chance Saloon.

There were no hitching posts at all, he realized, nor any horses; and the street was flanked by shiny, boxy wagons with tiny wheels. They were brightly painted, and the tiny wheels made him think they must be toys.

As long as he walked through the town, Miguel kept his eyes on the ground to avoid looking at the unrecognizable world around him. To let himself take notice of it would dull his instincts and make him lose his way.

This *was* Los Reales—Dorthea had told him so. All he had to do was let his tracker's sense of direction lead him where he needed to go.

He kept to the shadows and moved at a moderate pace. He didn't want to arouse suspicion, which he knew a running man invariably did.

But once he reached the outskirts, he began to run.

Again he had to rely on instinct and his sense of direction alone. All the subtle signs he usually counted on to find his way through the trackless desert were gone although, this time, not because of snow.

The rocks and boulders had somehow shifted their positions. The towering, man-limbed saguaros no longer spoke to him in a language he understood. The desert floor beneath his feet *looked* the same, but he knew it was not.

Just as Los Reales was the same, but not the same.

Even as Dorthea was the same, yet not. Even as her name was the same, but also different. For the brief moment he had clasped her in his arms, she had felt the same, even dressed in odd, men's clothing as she was.

Then her strong arms, developed by years of her insistence on riding as she pleased, despite her mother's warnings that no one would ever marry a woman with arms like a ranch hand, had pushed him away.

His body quickened, as always, at the very thought of her.

But then he recalled the way her lively blue eyes had looked at him not with passion but with pity.

She had looked at him with a stranger's eyes.

Madre de Dios, what was happening?

His head was filled with bits and pieces of memories that made no sense to him. At least, he called them memories—he didn't know what *else* to call them. They were like dreams, with no beginning and no end, and nothing that connected them one to the other.

He remembered a blinding snowstorm, men on horseback. He even remembered running, the way he was running now, but there was snow on the ground, and the sound of horses' hooves behind him.

And then a shiver of pure terror ran up his spine. He remembered children's voices, singing as they had sung tonight outside Dorthea's window. They had been singing . . . singing Christmas songs . . . when the men came.

What men?

Lifting his eyes heavenward, for some reason he did not understand, he half expected to see the twisted branches of a mesquite directly above him.

Why?

He shuddered again, fearing the answer almost as much as he feared the not knowing.

Where did these memories come from? What did they mean?

Madre de Dios, what was wrong with his head, filled with visions he could neither remember nor forget?

Was he going crazy? Miguel wondered. He ran faster, trying to outrun the memories, but they pursued him like the thundering horses' hooves he imagined he could hear closing in on him.

At last he saw in the distance the Mission San Xavier del Bac—the White Dove of the Desert. It glowed whitely in the moonlight. He ran toward it as toward a sanctuary, achingly familiar, and the only familiar thing in a world turned suddenly upside down.

"FATHER SEBASTIANI? There's no one here by that name. I'm Father Kino. Perhaps I can be of assistance?"

"No, I must speak with Father Sebastiani. When will he return?"

"Well, I can't say, because I've never heard of the man. Let me check with my housekeeper, she's run this house for more years than I've been alive. Mrs. Quito," he called over his shoulder. "This young man is inquiring about a Father Sebastiani. Do you know someone by that name?"

A dark Indian woman shuffled to the door, wiping her hands on her apron. She poked at the wisps of hair that had escaped the bun at the back of her neck, and gave the question some thought. Then she turned to

Father Kino and rattled off a few sentences in a combination of Spanish and Papago that Miguel found hard to follow.

"She says no. She says she's been housekeeper at the rectory for forty years, and there's never been a priest here by that name."

Mrs. Quito tugged at Father Kino's sleeve, and rattled off another barrage of sentences.

"She says there was a Father Sebastiani here once. It was a long time ago. Her mother spoke of him. But she only passed on stories she'd heard from her own mother, many years before that. It's said among the Indians that this Father Sebastiani put a curse on the town of Los Reales after some cattlemen desecrated the church."

Miguel felt his blood run cold.

Again the snow swirled around him; again he saw the mounted cowboys and the rope they had thrown over a sturdy mesquite limb. He was afraid to look up, afraid he would see the mesquite branch again over his own head.

"Why...did they desecrate the church?" he whispered.

But he had a terrible suspicion that he already knew the answer.

Father Kino repeated the question to the old woman, then translated her words to Miguel.

"They hanged an innocent man—an Indian who had taken sanctuary on the altar, so the legend goes. Some say it was over water rights. Others say it was over a beautiful redheaded woman who loved the Indian against her family's wishes."

The priest paused, dismissing the story with a patronizing smile. "Of course, it's only a myth."

"When did this happen?" Miguel whispered.

Father Kino repeated the question to the old woman, who screwed her eyes shut and appeared to calculate carefully before she spoke.

"She says her grandmother was just a child then, and now she has been dead since Mrs. Quito herself was a child," the priest translated. "She says her grandmother was at the Mission the night the man was taken away. It happened on Christmas Eve, she says. One hundred years ago."

Chapter Three

Dallas swerved her pickup into the front yard of her father's house and came to a stop in a flurry of gravel just inches from the weathered old porch.

From his perch on a hard-backed chair tipped against the side of the house, Rooster McAllister rustled the pages of the newspaper he was reading and grunted.

She honked the horn. "Hi, Pa!" she called cheerfully.

Wearing boots and jeans and a fleece-lined denim jacket, for the early desert morning was still cool, Dallas jumped down from the cab. She stomped up the porch steps two at a time, picked up her father's empty coffee cup and disappeared into the house.

In the hallway that led to the kitchen, her eyes fell on a grouping of photographs tacked on the wall; tattered black-and-whites, faded sepia tones, ferrotypes, a few very old daguerreotypes. She had hung them there herself, a long time ago.

Shortly after her mother had divorced Rooster and gone away for good, nine-year-old Dallas had been whiling away a rainy afternoon in the attic. She had come across a steamer trunk full of old family pictures. It had seemed to the lonely little girl that she had found friends in the attic.

One in particular had caught her imagination and held it. The old daguerreotype was of a beautiful woman, grown up but still very young.

Dallas hadn't known who she was—some old relative, Rooster had told her—but the girl in the daguerreotype had become her best friend.

Dallas had spent hours fantasizing stories about her, having adventures with her, holding long and serious conversations with her. The girl, silent though she was, was still better company than the taciturn Rooster. Dallas had called her Dorie, which had been her mother's pet name for her.

They even looked a little alike, Dallas had liked to think, at least in the way of frizzy, flyaway hair that Dallas was sure had been as red as her own.

Beyond that, however, not even Dallas's hopeful eyes could see any resemblance. The girl's face was fine-boned and beautiful, while her own had the round, childlike features of a face still in the making.

Now, whenever she entered the house, Dallas's eyes went automatically to the picture, as if to say hello to her old friend.

Only occasionally did it occur to her that looking at the daguerreotype was like looking into a mirror.

A few minutes later Dallas returned to the porch, placed a steaming refill beside Rooster's chair, and settled herself on the top step.

From where she sat she could see in the distance a saguaro-studded desert of muted greens that gradually climbed to jagged foothills of brown and dusky purple. There were trails lined with mesquite and prickly pear and cholla cactus, and rocky washes where the early morning sun tinted the bleached rocks and sand to soft pastels—gentle lavenders, quiet blues, pale pinks.

"Why you gotta make so much racket?" her father complained from behind the paper. "A lady don't never make so much racket. A lady don't never drive hell-bent for leather, neither. Your ma'd be real disappointed."

That was her father's most frequent expression of disapproval. Dallas wondered why. Her mother had decamped twenty years ago, probably sick to death of Los Reales. She had been raised by her stern and uncommunicative father, who had brought her up half housekeeper, half hired hand, and took it for granted that the lady part would somehow come later.

"Well, Pa, one thing you know for sure about me— I'm no lady!" She looked up at the front page of the *Los Reales Gazette,* which hid her father's face. Only 10 Shopping Days Left Until Christmas warned the red letters just above the paper's banner.

"Only ten shopping days left until Christmas, Pa," she told him, pushing the paper upward with one finger until she could see his face. She grinned teasingly. "Have you gotten me a present yet?"

"No, I ain't got your present yet," he growled. What remained of his red hair bristled like the coxcomb he was nicknamed for. "I ain't got money for such foolishness, girl. You know that."

He had said the same thing every year since she was a little girl, and every year it was truer than the year before. Rooster McAllister was land poor.

Once it had been good land, with water enough for the tribes who had lived on it for centuries and the occasional white settlement. But then the cattlemen came. They commandeered the wells and overgrazed the fragile desert environment. Now it was land that required fifty acres to raise a single head of livestock.

But Rooster McAllister held on to it. It had been McAllister land for well over one hundred years, and he wasn't going to be the first to break up the family's holdings.

So he waited for the water to come back, just as his father and grandfather had waited. And it broke his heart and his spirit, just as it had broken theirs.

Of course, if it was up to her, Dallas wouldn't have sold the ranch, either. She was a McAllister, too, and she loved the land as much as her father did. Not for the sparse grazing land it offered cattle, but for its enduring beauty, its timelessness, its promise of immortality.

There was something else, too, even beyond the tenuous taproot that bound her to McAllister land.

When she walked on this land, or in the town of Los Reales, she felt as though she was waiting for something.

What that might be, she had no idea. There were times she wondered restlessly if all she was waiting for was life to pass her by. There was no future here, she told herself time and time again; still she waited.

"I just came by to see if you need anything done, Pa," Dallas said.

"I can do what needs doing on my own land, girl," Rooster replied curtly. "What *you* need to do is be back in town tending to your job, getting criminals off the streets."

Here it comes again, Dallas groaned, but she couldn't resist rising to the bait. "You mean, like the de Pimas, Pa?"

"Sure, the de Pimas. And their friends. And any other bad elements."

"But not the McAllisters, right, Pa? Not any of our friends?"

"Don't start with me, Dorothy Alice," Rooster warned. "You know what I mean."

She knew what he meant.

According to half the townspeople, whenever a McAllister was in a position of power, it was incumbent on them to harass, annoy, and impoverish the de Pima family in every way possible—legal, quasi-legal, or downright illegal.

According to the *other* half, naturally, any de Pima who got in the position to do so had to do the same to the McAllisters.

Her father had expected Dallas to use her position as justice of the peace to establish McAllister dominance in Los Reales. He was bitterly disappointed when she'd refused.

"I'm sick of this blood-feud stuff, Pa," she had told him. "And I'm going to do everything I can to bring an end to it. After all this time, no one's heart is really in it, anyway—no one even remembers how it started anymore."

"That ain't true, Dorothy Alice. They're bad, those de Pimas. They always *been* bad—" Rooster had retorted before she'd cut him off.

"And they say the same thing about us!" she'd stormed.

Yes, she knew what he meant, all right, she reflected bitterly, and she hated it. But she also knew that they had been over this ground too often to have anything new to say.

"Truce, Pa," Dallas said now. She propped her forearms on her upraised knees and wrapped her hands around the warm coffee mug. "I've got a free day, that's all. I know you fired Two Bits and Hoohah last week—"

"Both of 'em useless as tits on a boar hog," Rooster interjected.

"Maybe. But you know you can't do all the work yourself." It was an indirect reference to Rooster's stiffened leg, the result of a fall from a horse four years ago, but as usual, the old man refused to acknowledge it.

"I don't need help," Rooster growled irritably. With brusque gestures, he refolded his newspaper and shoved it under one arm, then got to his feet and hobbled awkwardly into the house.

"The day I can't run my own spread is the day I dig a hole in the ground and bury myself in it." Dallas heard him muttering.

Under her breath, she muttered a few choice words of her own. "Okay, Pa," she called. "I'll be going then."

"Hold on a minute," Rooster grumbled from the dim interior. "I s'pose if you ain't got nothin' better to do with yourself, you might's well take your truck and drive the fence line back of the south forty. Ain't got around to it for a while."

Dallas grinned. "Sure, Pa."

"And, er, seein' as how you're gonna be out there, anyway, you might's well pitch a couple dozen hay bales over the fence."

"Sure, Pa." Still smiling, Dallas pushed herself up from the porch and headed for her pickup.

THE FENCES around the south forty were in perfect condition, mute evidence that Two Bits and Hoohah had been better at their jobs than her father had given them credit for.

She wondered why he had really fired the grizzled old hired hands—because he was dissatisfied with their work, or because he could no longer afford to keep them on?

Finding no fences to mend, Dallas forked bales of hay to the livestock until she worked up a sweat, but when she had finished, it wasn't even noon yet. She climbed back into her truck and took a long drink from the water bottle no desert dweller ever traveled without.

The day stretched out before her interminably.

She had to keep herself too busy to think, because every time she let her guard down, her thoughts kept returning to the bizarre encounter in her courtroom. She had learned that last night, when she'd spent hours tossing and turning in her bed, trying to remember where and when she might have met Miguel de Pima before.

Miguel de Pima.

The stranger who thought he knew her.

The stranger who drew from her a startling physical response, as though her body recognized him even while her mind was drawing a blank.

The stranger who thought they had planned some kind of future together. Which was ridiculous, of course. Dallas had never in her life known anyone she cared for enough to marry, not even during the few years she had lived in Phoenix, sampling life in the city and discovering that it smothered her.

She was worried about him, Dallas finally decided. That was all. He had seemed so disoriented, and she had just let him walk out into the night, a de Pima wandering unaware and unprotected through McAllister territory! It was her job as Los Reales's chief peace officer to make sure he had made it safely to his destination. Wasn't it?

It was her job to explain to him the realities of life in this outlaw town. It was more than her job, it was her duty!

Having summoned up enough reasons to do what she had intended to do all along, Dallas shifted her pickup into four-wheel drive and lurched overland across the rough terrain toward the Mission.

FIRST, SHE WENT to the administrative office, located in the old convent that had long ago been the Indian school. She found Father Kino hard at work behind his computer.

"Yes," he replied in answer to her question. "I did have a visitor very late last night. A young Indian. Said his name was de Pima, but I didn't recognize him, and as you know, most of the de Pima families belong to this parish."

"Do you know where he went when he left here?" Dallas asked.

"He didn't leave here. I let him stay the night in the sacristy." Father Kino smiled a little sheepishly seemingly at a loss to explain his own behavior. "I'm supposed to keep the church locked at night—a shame, isn't it? What *is* a church, after all, if not a sanctuary for those lost and in trouble? But this man..."

There were so many drifters these days. Father Kino felt compassion toward all of them—all the nameless men and, nowadays, even women who belonged nowhere.

But this one, possibly lost but not in trouble—Father Kino was sure—was different. He didn't ask for help; he didn't even appear to realize he needed it. Rather, Father Kino had the most preposterous sensation the young Indian had something to offer *him.*

"This man... There was just something about him," the priest finished. His sheepish smile was replaced by a frown as baffled as the one that had been in the young Indian's eyes. "I... simply couldn't tell him... there was no room at the inn."

He paused, then cleared his throat in a back-to-business manner. "If you want to see him, he's in the church. He's been there all morning."

MIGUEL WAS SEATED in the first pew.

Wearing whole and clean clothing, obviously borrowed from Father Kino, he was motionless, and Dallas sensed that he had been that way for a long time. She walked around the few sightseers, who were studying the baroque richness of the old church's interior, and slid in beside him.

"Hello, Miguel," she said instead of the "Mr. de Pima" she had intended to say.

"Dorthea. *Dorothy Alice.*" His voice was grave.

"Dallas, please. No one calls me Dorothy Alice except my father, and that's only when he's angry with me."

Miguel smiled, but the smile didn't reach his somber eyes.

Dallas looked up at the altar. The women of the Papago tribe, following an Indian Christmas tradition that dated back three hundred years, had dressed the statues of the saints in colorful satin robes. Two angels suspended over the altar were clothed in fine, starched lace, and their hands held a green satin banner that bore the words Gloria In Excelsis Deo.

The steps leading to the altar were banked with potted poinsettias, as lush and red as those that bloomed wild in the desert at this time of year. On either side of the steps, two life-sized lions, covered with gold leaf, were draped with red velvet capes and gold braid.

"Isn't the altar beautiful this time of year?" she said, unable to come up with any better way to open a conversation with a strange man who thought last night that she was his fiancée. Who knew, she wondered, what he might think her to be today?

"Yes," Miguel agreed. "But I remember it very differently."

"Oh? In what way?"

"When I was last here, there were no benches. Everyone stood, except the old people, and they sat on blankets on the floor. And the murals were more colorful. There was much gold here—the carved columns were covered with it. So were many of the saints.

"And Saint Cecilia and Saint Catherine—" he referred to two headless statues that graced the portal, the former on the upper story, the latter on the lower "—had heads."

Dallas laughed. "Well, the paint has lasted remarkably well, considering it's over two hundred years old. Saint Cecilia and Saint Catherine lost their heads, so the Papago say, when the Apaches roped them and pulled them off during their last raid . . . in the late nineteenth century."

She looked at Miguel strangely. "You couldn't possibly remember that. You must be thinking about stories you heard when you were growing up."

"I *do* remember these things," he repeated in a low, tense voice. "And I believe it is not from stories I have heard."

Uncomfortable, Dallas tried to bring the conversation back to reality. "How long has it been since you've eaten? Not since yesterday at least, I bet. You must be starved. Why don't you let me buy you lunch?"

"I . . . cannot remember when I ate last. I think it must have been a very long time ago." He looked at her gravely. "Yes, I am hungry. Thank you." Like a sleepwalker, or a figure moving in slow motion, Miguel stood and edged sideways out of the pew.

Now the question facing Dallas was, where to take him?

There was no demilitarized zone in Los Reales. Miguel might feel more comfortable in de Pima territory, but in a south-side café, would she be the justice of the peace or just another despised McAllister?

She finally decided on the Santa Fe Café, on the McAllister side of town.

Tongues might wag if she were seen there in the company of a de Pima, but at least it was the sort of quiet, family café that wouldn't permit blood to be spilled on its linoleum floors.

"I KNOW THIS PLACE," Miguel said after the hostess, eyebrows raised a little, showed them to the last booth at the rear. Beside them, an artificial Christmas tree twinkled merrily.

"You should. It's been here forever." It was, in fact, a piece of Los Reales history, a replica of the old Santa Fe Line train station that had once occupied the site.

"But I remember it . . . differently. It was rundown. There was a boardwalk in front and telegraph office in the back. They did not serve food. And the train to Tucson and Santa Fe stopped here once a week—"

A waitress appeared. "A hamburger and an ice tea," Dallas ordered. "You, Miguel?"

"A steak?" he said, looking quizzically at the waitress as if to determine whether he had said the right thing. She nodded. "And a beer?" he added, waiting again for her nod.

"Miguel." Dallas's voice was firm, but gentle. "I know this must be a terribly difficult time for you. You don't know who you are or where you came from. You don't seem to remember any of your past life before you came to Los Reales. That can happen sometimes when a man gets lost in the desert, or stays up in the mountains too long."

She waited to see if he identified with either of these scenarios.

After a silent moment, she continued. "Maybe you've been injured. Maybe you have amnesia. But whatever it is, there are doctors who can help you. Not here in Los Reales, but there are in Tucson—I'd be happy to help you find one."

"A difficult time, more than you know," Miguel repeated with an ironic twist to his thin, straight lips. "You are very good, Dor—Dallas—to be willing to do so much for one you believe to be a stranger. But I have learned what is wrong with me, and it is not a problem a doctor can cure."

Lowering his voice to no more than a whisper, Miguel leaned closer. "Dallas, do you believe that people can come back to life after they have already died?"

Dallas was startled. Whatever she had expected, it definitely was not that. "Some people believe it...."

"Do *you?*"

"Some religions teach it," she began carefully. "But me? No. No, I can't say that I do."

"I never did, either. Not until now."

Dallas looked at him uneasily. "What do you mean?"

Miguel reached across the table and covered one of her hands with his own. "I mean myself. I mean that I, myself, have returned to life, Dor—*Dallas*. One hundred years after I was murdered."

Chapter Four

Dallas shivered and pulled her hand away. "Don't talk that way," she said uneasily.

"Does it frighten you?"

"It takes more than a hallucination to frighten me," she replied firmly. "But it does concern me that if you convince yourself of this, you might not seek the help you need."

Miguel smiled.

It was the first true smile she had seen from him, Dallas noted somewhere in the back of her mind, and it was very endearing. She liked the way it lightened the somber expression he usually wore, and made his dark eyes shine. He was a very attractive man; she reiterated her first impression of last night. She hoped that after he got this *identity* problem cleared up, she would have many more opportunities to make him smile.

"It is good of you to care so much about someone you met not twenty-four hours ago," he said. "Last night I am sure I must have looked loco, like some drifter that got his brain scrambled by the sun. But you trusted me.''

''What on earth makes you think I trusted you?''

''Well, because you reached for your weapon, but you didn't draw it on me.''

''W-weapon?'' she sputtered, surprised and a little embarrassed by his perception, because she had always made it a point to keep the 12-gauge out of sight. No sense inviting trouble, she reasoned, but no sense taking chances, either. ''How did you know I had a weapon?''

''Dorthea's father was a judge. He always kept a shotgun behind his desk.''

''What does this Dorthea's father have to do with me?'' Dallas demanded. ''I don't even know these people you keep talking about. Besides, I'm a justice of the peace, not really a judge.''

''He wasn't really a judge, either. He just appointed himself one—judge, jury, *and* executioner. And he had plenty of his own people to back him up.''

Miguel lifted his shoulders and then let them fall. ''And who was going to challenge him? After he'd hung enough men so that everyone else in the territory knew he meant business, no one even thought about trying anymore. The Hangin' Judge, they called him.''

''But what does that have to do with *my* keeping a gun behind my desk,'' Dallas persisted. *''If,''* she added as an afterthought, ''in fact I *do* keep a gun behind my desk.''

"The Hangin' Judge knew how the town hated him, and he knew he wouldn't have a chance if someone really wanted to kill him. How much less of a chance would a beautiful woman have, in a town filled with gamblers and outlaws and hired guns?"

Dallas bristled. "This town isn't filled with gamblers and outlaws—" she began, then stopped short.

Wasn't it? What of the mayhem at 2:00 a.m., when the bars closed and oozed their sodden patrons out into the streets? What about the illegal gambling down in Big Lil's back room?

"That's beside the point," she finished lamely. "I don't *know* this judge, nor his daughter, whom you've obviously gotten mixed up with me."

"But you *do* know him. His likeness hangs in your office."

"His likeness?" Dallas was bewildered. Only two photographs hung in her office, and she was sure the governor of Arizona had never been involved in the sort of misconduct Miguel described. "You mean that old daguerreotype of Judge McAllister? But he lived over...over a hundred years ago!"

"Yes, Judge McAllister. *The McAllister*. His blood runs in you. And so does Dorthea's."

Miguel recaptured her hand and held it more firmly. "The McAllister murdered me, Dallas. On Christmas Eve, one hundred years ago. He hanged me because I was an Indian and I had dared to love his daughter— his daughter who looked so much like you."

Dallas shivered. Stalkers reasoned like this, she thought uneasily. Last night she had concluded absolutely that Miguel was not dangerous; but this particular fantasy convinced her more than ever that he needed help. "That would have been . . . Dorthea?"

"Yes."

"And that would have been . . . a hundred years ago?"

"Yes."

Her brows furrowed thoughtfully, Dallas found herself trying to think of something that teased at her memory, hovering just beyond her ability to recall.

Miguel's story was vaguely familiar. It reminded her of something she vaguely recalled having heard, a very long time ago. She couldn't even remember where or when she had heard it; but in looking back, it seemed now that it had been some sort of old Papago myth.

Still frowning, she tried to reconstruct the details from the bits and pieces of her memory.

The myth concerned an Indian, she thought now, who had been framed and executed for a crime he hadn't committed. He had been charged with stealing, or being a horse thief, or something like that. But his real crime had been in falling in love with a woman not of his own kind, for which the woman's father had seen to it that he was hanged.

Could it be possible that Miguel had heard that myth, too, maybe when he was growing up? And now, for some reason—an injury? A subconscious need?—something had twisted around in his mind and made him think the myth was true? And that it was about *him?*

It was possible! It was more than possible; it made perfect sense!

Dallas turned their clasped hands over so that rather than his holding hers, she gripped his instead.

"Oh, Miguel," she said earnestly. "Listen to what you're saying! Don't you realize how crazy—irrational—this sounds? I don't know why you're dreaming up these things, but they're not real. They're nothing more than figments of your imagination—hallucinations. You're ill, Miguel. You need help. Please, let me take you to Tucson—"

Suddenly a shadow fell across the booth. A black Stetson hat struck the table between them with an authoritarian thump. It was held there by a large hand that Dallas recognized instantly by the ornate, silver and turquoise ring on the fourth finger.

Her head jerked up and her heart sank. Leaning over the booth was a tall, leathered rancher whom she religiously went out of her way to avoid. His bulk hovered menacingly over herself and Miguel.

"Afternoon, Dallas. This man botherin' you?"

"Wyatt," she acknowledged. "No. As you can see, we're having lunch together. Miguel, this is Wyatt Slocum. Wyatt, Miguel."

Her voice was curt, but Wyatt didn't take the hint. He propped one booted foot on the edge of the vinyl cushion where she sat, then draped his forearm on his upraised knee.

"Way-ell, that's okay, then. Business, is it? One of your perpetrators, huh?" Tickled by his own quip, Wyatt snickered unpleasantly. "That it, Mee-gel? You one of her troublemakers? Or you one of her lawyer friends—" he pronounced it *fra-yands* "—from Tucson?"

"Her friend, yes," Miguel replied neutrally. "But I'm not from Tucson."

"Way-ell," Wyatt drawled. "You gotta be from *some*wheres else, else you woulda known your kind's not welcome here."

Dallas half rose in her seat. "Wyatt!" she snapped through clenched teeth. "Leave! Now!"

"I'll do that, Dallas. But maybe you outta remember who you are. And who *he* is. You know the funny way things happen to folks from the south side that stray over to this side of town."

Wyatt Slocum tightened his thick fingers around the crown of his Stetson, lifted it from the table and clamped it on his head. Then, giving Dallas a reproving tsk and ignoring Miguel altogether, he lowered his booted foot to the floor. He sauntered over to the bar, where he kept a skeptical eye on them from behind the artificial Christmas tree.

"That man is still watching us," Miguel informed Dallas.

"That man is a jerk," Dallas stated unequivocally. Still, she thought uneasily after the waitress had delivered their lunch, until she could persuade him to go with her to Tucson, she'd better tell Miguel the unpleasant facts of life in Los Reales.

"So THAT'S THE WAY IT IS," Dallas said, finishing. "This blood feud's been going on for as long as anyone can remember. Lots of folks have been hurt by it over the years. But the whole town keeps at it, and no one has any energy left for anything else. It's as though we're stuck in a time warp—we keep repeating the same old scripts over and over again, and we can't seem to get it right."

They sat on Dallas's tiny patio, beneath baskets of greenery that she fussed over constantly to keep alive. Right beside the sliding-glass door was a potted ficus tree; decorated with twinkling red lights shaped like chili peppers, it was what Dallas liked to call her Christmas tree.

Because Dallas couldn't come up with any other place where they could converse uninterrupted, she had decided to invite Miguel to her condo in the Gulf Winds Condominium Complex.

No gulf wind had ever found its way to Los Reales, she was certain; it was just some real estate developer's ploy to make buyers overlook the parched landscaping and think of things cool and refreshing.

She had lived in the Gulf Winds Condominium Complex for more than five years and hardly knew her neighbors. No one went outdoors much, not even the children. They spent most of their time in their air-conditioned units with their televisions on.

That, plus the fact that her own unit faced the seldom-used pool area, with its tired-looking gardens and its sandy patches of desert scrub grass, made her decide that her home was as discreet a place as any to carry on a private and uninterrupted conversation with Miguel.

Today, however, two small boys were sailing paper boats on the surface of the pool. Alongside them stood their mother. All three gawked at Dallas's small patio, and at her guest, who obviously belonged on the other side of town.

"And no one remembers how the feud thing got started?" Miguel asked.

Dallas shook her head. "Do you know that old Papago story, where all the tribe's cornfields became poisoned, except for one very small one?"

"Tell me."

"Well, the poisoned corn tasted exactly like any other, but it made the people who ate it go insane. So the chief went to the shaman and asked what they should do. And the shaman thought about it, and then he said, 'Let the poisoned corn be eaten so that at least the people will not die. But feed the good corn to a few, so that there will be someone who remembers we are insane.'"

"I have never heard that before, but I understand its meaning. You are saying that no one in Los Reales got the good corn."

"Exactly. It's like there's something in the food. Like the fields are built on a nuclear dump site or something. And we eat the food because it's all we have. And it's made us insane, but there's no one who remembers that."

Miguel cocked his head quizzically. "What is a nuclear dump site?"

Dallas looked at him with surprise, then understood. Since they hadn't known about nuclear waste one hundred years ago, she guessed that Miguel's delusions wouldn't permit him to remember the words now.

At least his fantasy was consistent, she thought almost affectionately, recalling how astonished he had been by her truck. He'd wanted to drive it, and did a very credible job of not seeming to know the first thing about it.

He had learned very quickly, though. It was a lot like riding a horse, he said, only the seat was much more comfortable and you could get out of the weather.

He'd been astonished by the wide, smooth roads leading into and out of Los Reales, too, and by the tall streetlights—he wondered how the lamplighters were able to get to the top to light them.

She laughed inwardly, imagining the way he would react if she were to turn on her television.

Miguel might be delusional, she thought, but when she allowed herself to forget that, she found that she enjoyed his company more than any man she had ever known.

And she had to admit it wasn't due to his conversation alone.

These were not feelings she had experienced often in her life, and they made her decidedly uncomfortable, but uncomfortable in a way that made comfort the last thing in the world she wanted.

Just being near him—across a booth in the Santa Fe Café, even across the few concrete feet of her patio—made her feel exquisitely...*female.* She was more aware of her body—how the denim of her jeans rubbed against her skin, the way the silky texture of her bra caressed her breasts like the gentlest of fingers. She also had to admit that, whether near him, or as far away as across her courtroom, she couldn't escape her acute awareness of him as a man.

Unlike most men, Miguel didn't treat her as though he were a cowboy and she a maverick filly he was testosterone-bound to ride—the way, say, Wyatt did, every time she had the misfortune to run into him.

And she was willing to bet that Miguel didn't expect to end up in bed with her tonight, either, just because she had invited him into her home. Although oddly enough, she didn't find that thought unappealing.

Cherished. She remembered the quaint, old-fashioned word, and she remembered the fleeting feeling. She wondered if he could make her feel that way again.

"It sounds like *you* ate the good corn," Miguel pointed out. "Why did your family not pass this insanity on to you?"

"I don't know. It wasn't for lack of trying, though, I can tell you that! I just somehow always knew it was wrong. And stupid. My father and I have had many a knock-down-drag-out over it, but nothing ever gets settled. Every time it comes up, we end up running on the same old treadmill again, going nowhere.

"Anyway, Miguel, I wanted you to know so you can protect yourself. People around here seem to have a sixth sense about who belongs where."

Dallas stopped speaking for a moment, then sighed. "The thing is that every other town in the Tucson Valley has dealt with the same problems and gotten past them. Life's never been easy out here, and most people finally learned that if we don't stand together, we'll fall apart. But not us. Not Los Reales."

She banged her palm on the aluminum arm of the lounge she sat in. "Why *not* Los Reales!" she exclaimed in frustration.

In the one-hundred-plus years between its ignominious beginnings—a miserable settlement of drifters, fugitives and malcontents huddled against the walls of the presidio like dozens of other similar settlements—and today, something had gone dreadfully wrong with Los Reales.

Some towns had withered and died, and some of those had become ghost towns, meccas for intrepid tourists seeking the Old West. Others had blossomed into urban or agricultural centers. Only Los Reales squatted like a lost creature in the middle of the desert, too tough to die, but not tough enough to get on with living.

Dallas shot a glance at Miguel. She wondered how much of what she'd told him he had understood.

How much could he relate to the problems of the twentieth century when he believed he had lived and died in the nineteenth? It was obvious that he had a past of *some* kind in this town, but it was also obvious that he was totally out of touch with the reality of today.

In the gathering dark, the automatic security floodlights around the pool switched on, and in the sudden light, she saw that his eyes were fixed on her. Suddenly shy, she scraped her aluminum chair across the concrete floor and rose reluctantly.

"It's just about dark," she announced unnecessarily, as if he couldn't have figured that out for himself. "Let's go inside and I'll rustle us up some coffee, and then I'd better drive you back to the Mission."

"I do not want to trouble you. I can get myself back to the Mission."

"It's going to be cold tonight," Dallas demurred, more than a little afraid that he might just walk into the desert and out of her life. "I'll be glad to run you back, no trouble at all—"

Suddenly she stopped midstep. In the process of reaching to open the sliding-glass patio door, her hand froze.

Her eyes, fixed on her reflection in the glass, widened to incredulous circles. Behind the door, the lights were off, and she could see herself in the glass as clearly as if in a mirror.

Her own wide eyes stared back at her.

She saw her windblown, orange-red hair, her red plaid Western shirt with the sleeves pushed up to her elbows, her slim-fitting Levi's, her gray, ostrichskin boots. She saw the entire patio reflected down to the smallest detail in the thick, plate glass—

But she did *not* see Miguel!

Slowly she turned, reassuring herself of his size, his shape, his presence behind her; but when she looked toward the glass again, he was not there.

Her heart began to pound. "Miguel," she breathed, the word coming out a choked whisper. "What's going on...?" Turning again, she stared up at him with bewildered eyes, then slowly, warily, began to back away.

Miguel had not even noticed his lack of a reflection. He had been too preoccupied with watching Dallas and the way her lush female curves filled out the odd, but not unflattering, men's clothing she wore.

Now he looked through the glass into the dark room, and he saw what she had seen. Or more specifically, what she had *not* seen. His eyes became as wide as hers.

Quickly he turned to face her. "Dallas, please! Do not be afraid..."

But she continued to edge away until she was blocked by the low adobe wall that surrounded the patio. "Who...who *are* you?" she whispered in the same strangled voice.

Miguel reached for her. "I have been trying to tell you—"

"Stop right there," Dallas warned, half an order, half a plea. She extended her arms, palms outward, as though to ward him off. "Please move away from the door."

As he slowly moved to the opposite side of the postage-stamp patio, Dallas edged toward the glass door, arms still raised defensively in front of her.

Then she stepped quickly inside, sliding the door shut and locking it with hands that shook.

"Go away! Please, just go away!" Dallas implored. Her voice bordered on hysteria.

On the other side of the glass—it might as well have been the other side of the world—Miguel stood alone in the glaring floodlights.

She is afraid of me, Miguel grieved, and the thought pierced his heart like a knife. She had thought he was crazy with his tale of having been murdered and returned to life one hundred years later.

Now she probably believed that *she* was the crazy one. How often, after all, do you invite into your home a man who casts no reflection?

Miguel considered the possibilities. Was he a ghost? No, for he could feel his own body, solid as any other man's.

Was this hell, then? The hell that Father Sebastiani had preached about so relentlessly?

If so, why was Dallas—Dorthea—in it? Dorthea was a saint; and when he was with her, he had been, too. They had never broken any laws of God or man, hard though that had been to resist in the brief stolen hours when their bodies had burned to obey laws far older than those of church or man.

But they *had* resisted, forced themselves to wait until their wedding day, which never came. The Mc-Allister had seen to that. So how could this be hell?

Maybe this was his own private hell, Miguel thought suddenly, where he was condemned to suffer the fires of desire for all eternity? Where he was condemned to yearn forever for Dorthea, but never, ever possess her?

Father Sebastiani had never spoken of separate hells, but it made sense to Miguel, at least as much sense as everything else that was happening to him.

He groaned. He had promised Dallas never to hurt her again, and now she was terrified, as she had every right to be.

So was he.

The wind picked up, carrying with it fine particles of sand that sprinkled like rain against the adobe walls of the Gulf Winds Condominium Complex.

Across the swimming pool Miguel saw a coyote, shadowed by the floodlights, skulk toward the water and then lower its muzzle to drink. When, he wondered with a vague sense of dread, had a coyote come so close to man? A hoot owl screeched—always a bad sign.

He shivered convulsively. The cold of the stonelike patio floor seeped through his boots the way the warm desert sand never did. An icy chill suddenly gripped his body, but he knew the chill had nothing to do with the rapidly falling temperature.

Miguel remembered racing two nights ago through the snow toward the old Mission, his body covered with cholla spines and blood, and the sound of horses' hooves thundering in his ears.

He remembered running there again last night, hoping that Father Sebastiani would have answers for the questions Miguel couldn't even put into words.

Now, for what was to him the third night in a row, he took to his heels, running like the wind toward the White Dove of the Desert, all the hounds of hell baying at his heels.

IN THE DISTANCE, he finally caught sight of the Mission. The only light inside was a single, yellow square in Father Kino's office.

It might have been the candle from Father Sebastiani's study, but Miguel knew it was not. It was Father Kino's study, and the light came from a glass lamp that turned itself on with a flick of a switch.

This priest worked late into the night, Miguel thought, just as Father Sebastiani had; it must be a never-ending task, this saving of souls.

Soundlessly, so as not to disturb Father Kino, Miguel entered the Mission through the kitchen door and went directly to the sacristy, where the compassionate priest had fashioned for him a makeshift bedroom. The room was like a monk's cell—narrow, with yellowed walls and a high ceiling now hidden in shadow. A small armoire stood in one corner, where hung Father Kino's vestments.

Miguel crossed to the window, also high and narrow, with mullions of wrought iron flaking rust at the edges. Throwing open the shutters, he gazed out at the familiar, yet not familiar, landscape.

Moonlight spilled mystically over the domes, the balustrated walls, the gated arches of the Mission. It gave the plastered adobe a cool, blue cast, unlike the warm cream color Miguel remembered.

The White Dove of the Desert was now painted white, Father Kino had told him last night in answer to his query; it was no longer hand-burnished with the mixture of cactus juice and lime that had once given it its natural patina.

There was an unearthly glow in the sky in the direction of the old cow town called Tucson. It looked like the light from a million lanterns. It wasn't fire, because smoke didn't blacken the skies and the undersides of the clouds didn't reflect the red of flames.

Yet it was something, creating light where there should be darkness.

Father Kino had also explained that.

"Is it a wildfire?" Miguel had asked.

"No," Father Kino had replied, looking at Miguel strangely. "That's the reflection from the city lights of Tucson."

Father Kino had answered many questions last night. Finally, noticing the strange expression on the priest's face, Miguel had stopped asking them.

What had happened to him?

The last thing he remembered was his hands tied behind his back, and the snow, the strange, unnatural snow, swirling around him.

The last thing he thought he would hear in this world was Dorthea, rocking back and forth on her knees in the snow, already keening for him.

The last thing he thought he would see was her bright, copper-colored hair falling like a dank shroud over her face, looking as red as blood against the pure, driven snow.

Then she was gone. And all that remained was the dark, hot, rapidly fading red behind his eyelids.

Tonight, as Miguel stood at the sacristy window and stared out across the desert where he had lived his life, he was reassured by its sameness. Different in its details, it was unchanged in its essence.

Except for the glowing dome of light over Tucson, it looked as though it hadn't even noticed the passing of one hundred years.

He could see the dark hulk of Sentinel Peak jutting up into the sky from the ridge of the Tucson Mountains. It had been a point of reference for anyone traveling in the desert.

Was it still? Could a man still take his angle off it and find himself where he'd wanted to go?

Did the desert that had been his home hold the answers to all his questions? And would the answers, when he found them, be more frightening than the not-knowing had been?

Miguel wondered.

Chapter Five

Only 9 More Shopping Days Left Until Christmas.

Dallas poured a second cup of coffee and tried to make sense of the newsprint that swam before her eyes. Pushing her hair back from her face, she downed most of the coffee in several long gulps that scalded her mouth, and waited for the caffeine to kick in.

She hadn't slept a wink.

For the first few hours she had been too unnerved to think at all. Huddled in a corner of the couch, she had stared fearfully at the drapes that covered the patio door, her eyes wide open and as blank as her mind.

Later, her brain had tried to rationalize, tried to convince her that she couldn't have seen what she'd thought she'd seen. Later still, shivering uncontrollably beneath a mound of blankets, she kept replaying the events of the evening, trying to figure out exactly when had she joined Miguel in his bizarre and fantastical delusion.

All through the long night, she relived the moment when she'd turned toward the glass patio door. She'd considered every nuance of that moment; every angle of light, every explanation, every possibility—even the unlikely one that she had wanted so much to relate to Miguel that she'd allowed herself to buy into his fantasy. But when that moment came, it was always the same.

One minute they had been discussing, like two normal people, the insanity of the long-standing blood feud in Los Reales; the next, they had slid off into some greater insanity where perfectly solid men didn't cast reflections.

She shuddered again, remembering.

She wondered if Miguel was still out there, waiting for her? She was half afraid he'd appear in her bedroom the way he'd appeared in the back of her courtroom, pass right through her door like a ghost and...and what?

Hurt her? Never! Whatever else he was—A lost soul still trying to come to terms with the fact of his own existence? A time traveler?—Dallas already sensed that he was a good and gentle man.

The laws of physics had been broken.

And they'd been broken right here on her patio by a very attractive and mysterious man who insisted he had died one hundred years ago. She felt she should call the state department, or the pope, or *any*one else who might know how to deal with this.

But of course she couldn't do that. First of all, how did one get through to the state department or the pope? She suspected it wouldn't be as simple as picking up a telephone.

Second, what would she say? No one would believe it. She could hardly believe it herself, and she had seen it. They would think she was as out of touch with reality as she'd thought Miguel to be.

Third, there was Miguel.

Abandoning all attempts to make sense of the newspaper, Dallas stood and walked to the patio door. She pulled the drape back just a little and peeked outside, as if making sure there were no surprises waiting for her. But the world looked exactly the same as it had the night before, which, all things considered, surprised her most of all.

The sun was brilliant in the empty blue sky. The air was so clear that it seemed to Dallas she could see all the way to the foothills of the Huachuca Mountains. Every saguaro, every palo verde, every occasional mesquite, stood out with crystalline clarity.

There was no indication, in this obscure corner of the world, that all the theories of scientists and all the writings of philosophers down through the ages had just been turned upside down.

What she now needed to know was *why*.

AFTER A SLOW MORNING in traffic court, Dallas drove out to her father's house. She never counted on old Rooster for wisdom, but today what she needed wasn't wisdom, but familiarity. What she needed was a good dose of the usual, the ordinary, the commonplace.

The key was under the doormat.

Letting herself in, she was greeted by the slight odor of wood smoke. A nickle-plated, pot-bellied wood stove was the only source of heat in the house, and ever since she was a little girl, it's faint, acrid odor had been the smell of security. Now, as then, she felt an immediate rush of the reassurance she needed.

She set about doing the familiar homey tasks she had always done in this house.

She assembled about a month's worth of newspapers scattered throughout the rooms, and deposited them in the burn barrel. She collected used coffee cups from every available surface and carried them into the kitchen, pausing on the way down the hallway to give the daguerreotype of Dorie a quick and automatic hello.

Then she prowled through the cupboards and fridge to see what she could rustle up for dinner.

A nice, square meal, she thought fondly as her mind fell into the comfortable old grooves of weighing and stirring and browning and pouring, and allowed itself to rest. Her father mainly fixed canned foods and TV dinners for himself, she knew, and often she suspected he skipped meals altogether.

Finally sliding his favorite hamburger casserole into the oven, she adjourned to the parlor, where she sank into her mother's old rocking chair, removed her boots and extended her feet toward the wood stove, and immediately fell asleep.

It could have been minutes or hours later when she woke, hearing her father's heavy footsteps on the porch. It was that uneven, three-legged walk that had jarred her awake, she thought, because it was the first unfamiliar thing about the house—Pa had never walked with a cane when she'd lived here.

Rooster stumped in without saying a word. He hung his coat on a hook by the door, then stamped out to the kitchen for his customary three fingers of whiskey. Only then did he sink into the easy chair on the other side of the wood stove and *harrumph* a recognition of Dallas's presence.

"Supper smells good," he said, as he'd said thousands of times before.

"I hope it *is* good," she returned, as she had equally as many times before.

"Ain't often I see you twice in two days," Rooster offered after downing one finger of his whiskey. "Gonna make a pest outta yourself, girl?"

"No, Pa. I just had some business out this way, that's all."

Silence fell. Lengthened. In the wood stove, a log fell and hissed.

"Well, I guess that casserole must be about done," Dallas announced after a while. She started to push herself up from the rocker.

"Wait a minute, Dorothy Alice," Rooster said, motioning her to sit back down.

Uh-oh, Dallas sighed inwardly. *Dorothy Alice. What's wrong now? I wonder.* She sat.

"I was up to town today," the old man began with irritating pomposity. "And I heard somethin' really set me back on my heels. The whole town's whisperin' about you, girl—sayin' you been runnin' around with a de Pima."

He paused and fixed her with a hard stare. "That true, Dorothy Alice?"

"Pa, it was just..." For a wild moment she was tempted to borrow from the suggestions Wyatt had made in the café, then decided not to bother; she'd never gotten away with lying in this house anyway.

C'mon, Dorothy Alice, she said to herself in her father's scolding tone. *You're twenty-nine years old, when are you going to start standing up to the old ba—man?* "Just a lunch, Pa. He's just a friend."

"You don't be needin' a de Pima for a friend. You're supposed to be clearin'em off the streets, not buyin'em lunch. Anyways, it's not just lunch the whole town's jawboning about. They also say someone saw him at your condo last night. Your ma wouldn't approve—"

Hating herself, Dallas, as usual, rose to the bait. "Pa, as far as I can recall, my mother left because she was sick and tired of eating, breathing and sleeping with the feud. And frankly, so am I!"

"They may've put you in charge of the court around here, girl, but you're still just a kid. You got a lot to learn. Nothin' good's ever come of McAllisters and de Pimas mixin', and nothin' ever will."

"Nothing's come from us *not* mixing, either, that's for sure!" Dallas exclaimed in frustration. "Look around you! I swear, Pa, don't you ever wonder why the world has passed us by? We have no jobs, no industry, nothing! We could have had a military base like Fort Huachuca. We could have had a flight training center like Marana. We could have tourist facilities and retirement communities like Tucson—we've got the same climate and the same unspoiled desert that they do. But we've got nothing, Pa, nothing!"

Dallas ran out of steam. Her voice fell. As she kept reminding herself, they had been over this many times before. "Don't you ever wonder why?" she finished dully.

"We got what we want—"

"You've got what you *deserve*," Dallas muttered under her breath.

"Don't go smart-mouthin' me, Dorothy Alice. Anyways, that ain't got nothin' to do with what I was talkin' about. I don't want to see any daughter of mine draggin' the family name through the mud."

Dallas leapt to her feet. She snatched up her canvas tote bag, then stormed to the door and out of it. She let it bang hard against the sagging doorframe. *I hope it splinters,* she thought furiously.

Then she poked her head back inside. "Don't let the casserole burn, Pa," she growled, sounding more like old Rooster than she would have liked to admit. "And there's another one in the freezer."

DURING THE DRIVE home, Dallas decided to stop at the Mission. In spite of her father, or perhaps because of him, she wanted to make sure this one de Pima, at least, was still safe.

She owed Miguel an apology. He was as much a victim of this incomprehensible cosmic joke as she was. More. But because she was afraid, because she had panicked, she'd turned him away from one of the only two places in town—in the whole world—where he should have been welcome.

She realized that if she was frightened by the bizarre, supernatural turn events had taken, Miguel must be even more so. He was the one who had to deal with it; she could, if she chose, just walk away.

No, it dawned on her as she came to a stop in front of the White Dove of the Desert, the only mission built by the Franciscan friars still in use as a parish church. No, she couldn't just walk away. Not any more.

"HE'S GONE," Father Kino said when she found him in the vestibule of the church, stacking hymnals in the book rack. "He left this afternoon."

A cold stone dropped into the pit of Dallas's stomach. "Do you happen to know...where he went?"

"Well, of course I do!" Father Kino laughed. "I helped him make the arrangements. He's gone to stay at Mrs. Quito's place in Los Reales. The farm's really been going downhill since old Beginio broke his arm, and to tell the truth, so has Mrs. Quito's cooking, now that she's been trying to do all the work herself.''

He looked more closely at the pallor of Dallas's face. ''What's wrong, Dallas? You look like you could use a pick-me-up. Come on over to my office, and I'll put on some coffee. Actually, I'm glad you dropped by. I had rather a...strange experience today, and I could use someone to talk to.''

Father Kino's office was more than just quiet. It seemed to absorb sound, as if its yellowed walls were lined with cotton. It put Dallas in mind of a confessional.

She leaned backward in a chair on one side of the carved ironwood desk that had been imported, so Father Kino informed her proudly, from Spain three hundred years ago.

On the opposite side of the desk, Father Kino leaned forward on his elbows, folding his hands as though in prayer and tapping them thoughtfully against his chin.

Between them, steam from two mugs of instant coffee rose in the air, then disappeared like smoke into fog.

''Dallas,'' the priest began slowly, ''what do you know about Miguel de Pima?''

''Well, not much,'' Dallas replied, surprised.

''Has he talked about himself at all? Where he came from, that sort of thing?''

''Well, not much,'' Dallas could only repeat. She wondered where Father Kino was heading.

"He hasn't said much to me, either. But he made some rather curious statements the night he arrived here—about the Mission, I mean, and about people who used to be here. Mainly, a Father Sebastiani, who was the resident priest here, oh, a long time ago." He frowned and looked at Dallas from beneath the single dark line of his brow.

"Yes, he mentioned that name, as a matter of fact, the night he came to my courtroom. But that's all he did, mention it. Do you know who this Father Sebastiani is?"

"I didn't," Father Kino replied. "But I do now. I drove up to the Heard Museum in Phoenix today— they keep all those archaeological archives up there, you know."

Dallas nodded.

"In the Southwest Room, I looked up everything they had on the Mission. Those old priests kept very precise records—marriages, births, deaths, agricultural statistics, and all of it written by hand." He shook his head in admiration. "They were a different breed in those days.

"Anyway, I read the journals of this Father Sebastiani. He was a stickler for detail. Something he wrote caught my attention—I can't seem to get it out of my mind."

He paused, his voice perplexed, as if he himself wasn't sure his words were going to make any sense.

"Well, he wrote about something that happened while he was here. It was hard to decipher, but then, these were on microfilm—the originals are probably easier to read, but they're kept in climate-controlled vaults, you know, to preserve them. And the handwriting was cramped—to save paper, no doubt. And then, of course, since it was written with a quill pen.''

These disclaimers out of the way, he continued. ''Yes, well, this Father Sebastiani wrote about a young Indian, a Papago, who was framed for a crime he didn't commit, and was dragged away from the altar of San Xavier's where he'd sought sanctuary. Ripped his hands right off the feet of Our Lord on the cross, so Father Sebastiani said, and hung him at the first tree they came to. Any of this sound familiar to you?''

Dallas shrugged, wide-eyed. ''It's an old Indian myth, isn't it? I've heard the story, but I don't know much about it.''

''Well, I don't expect you would. You people on the north side don't spend as much time with the Indians as I do. Actually it *is* an old Indian myth. But not according to this Father Sebastiani.

''He says he saw it all. He begged for the young Indian's life, but the murderers just laughed at him. And as he tells it, he called upon God to put a curse on the murderers and their children for generations to come.''

He and Dallas looked at each other across the desk, his eyes narrowed and confounded beneath his furrowed brows, hers as wide and blue as they had been on the patio the night before.

Then he leaned backward in his swivel chair, which squeaked, dispelling the echoes of violence and death that filled the room.

"Of course," he added briskly, "keep in mind that he wrote this many years later, long after it was supposed to have happened. He was quite old by then, maybe senile. He could have forgotten some of the details, or even confused them with some similar Indian story." Having shared the writings of the friar long gone, Father Kino now seemed overly eager to discredit them.

"Did this old priest happen to mention the name of the man who was hung?"

"No."

"Did he mention the name of the town where the conflict started?"

Father Kino looked as confounded as he had at the beginning of his story. "Yes," he replied slowly. "Yes. It was Los Reales."

For a long time after Dallas had gone, the priest remained in his study, pondering the strange case of Miguel de Pima.

Perhaps, he thought, the young Indian had heard of the myth and had somehow created from it a fantasized identity of his own.

Miguel de Pima didn't strike him as a man suffering with a mental illness. But certainly it was a possibility—the human mind was susceptible to so many aberrations not fully understood even by those who claimed to study these matters.

It was the *only* palatable possibility, Father Kino concluded finally. Especially seeing as how the church, in these secular times, preferred not to have to deal with the "embarrassment" of miracles.

Still, somehow, the explanation, plausible though it was, now sat like a bout of indigestion on Father Kino's conscience.

Chapter Six

Although it was dark, and therefore not the safest thing to do, Dallas left the Mission and drove directly to the small farmhouse where Father Kino had told her the Quitos lived.

She seldom went to the south side, and never after sunset.

Eyes she couldn't even see seemed to watch her from the shadows. The streetlights illuminated men and boys loitering on the street corners—sometimes several, sometimes only one—waiting for trouble, no doubt. Or else looking for it.

Loitering. A misdemeanor punishable by probation and a fine, *if* the Los Reales cops had been willing to get out of their cruisers after dark to cite the offenders. Which they were not.

Her hair must stand out like a red flag in these dark streets, she thought tensely, announcing to one and all that she didn't belong here. As justice of the peace, she felt irritated by the intimidation; as a woman, she felt vulnerable.

At last, having driven through much of the south side, Dallas located the Quitos' nondescript clapboard farmhouse, identical to the several others that lined this dark country road.

As she pulled to a stop, she saw the front curtains part a little, and a disembodied head peek through the opening. Then another head appeared above the first and quickly vanished. Immediately, the front door flew open and Miguel came outside.

"What are you doing here?" he said, leaning into the passenger window as she touched the control button that rolled it down. "You know it isn't safe for a woman after dark."

"Not for a McAllister woman, anyway," she replied. She slid across the seat and jumped to the ground. "Mind if I come in?"

Miguel didn't mind, but it was obvious that the Quitos did. The family was seated around the chrome dinette set in the kitchen, halfway through their evening meal.

Mrs. Quito and her husband, Beginio, put down their forks and folded their hands nervously in their laps. They threw furtive glances toward the front window, as if expecting the curtains to fall away any minute and reveal to the whole neighborhood their unwelcome visitor.

Even the two small grandchildren who lived with them transferred their attention from their plates to the first real live McAllister monster they had ever set eyes on.

Probably expected me to have horns and tail, Dallas said to herself, remembering her own expectations about southsiders before she had ever met one.

It was a relief when Miguel finished with the introductions. He led her to the small bedroom he occupied at the rear of the house and pulled the door shut behind them.

"Why did you come here?" he asked gravely.

"I had to. I had to talk to you."

Dallas walked to the middle of the room, then turned to face him. "Miguel, I want to apologize for the way I acted last night. I know I just . . . abandoned you out there, and I'm so sorry."

"You believe me, then?"

"It's incredible, and I can't begin to explain it, but yes. Yes, I do. *Now.* But last night I was so scared, I didn't know what to think—I didn't know what to do."

"I understand." Miguel issued a token smile. "It is not every day that you invite a ghost into your home. You did not abandon me, Dallas."

Crossing his arms, he leaned dejectedly on one shoulder against the closed door. "But I think that maybe God has."

"What do you mean?"

He shrugged, looking angry and baffled. "For what purpose am I *here?*"

"You don't know?"

"I know nothing! Only that one moment I was mounted on a horse with a noose around my neck, and

I heard a shot, and I knew I was going to die. And
then . . . I was here."

"And you don't remember anything in between?"

"There was . . . the wind. And voices. Cries." He
hesitated. "Many voices crying. They came from far
away, like . . . echoes. And then they would be gone.
There was the sand . . . shifting . . ." He shook his head
in frustration. "No. No, I remember nothing."

"Many voices crying," Dallas repeated thoughtfully. "Life for your people was bad in those years.
The Indian Wars ended. Then the tribes were con-
fined to reservations—the Apache to Fort Apache
about the turn of the century, I think, and the Papago to several smaller ones at Sells and Ok-chin and
San Xavier about 1911. The other villages are gone."

"Gone!" Miguel exclaimed in disbelief. Then he
looked at Dallas for verification. "Gone?"

She nodded unhappily. "One hundred years is a
very long time," she said softly.

"But then, truly there is no reason for me to be
alive! Life is meaningless to me—my home is gone, my
family is gone. Dorthea is gone. I have no one—"

The pain in his voice cut Dallas to the quick. "You
have me. I'll help you."

"Ah, no, Dallas. You are kind, but we both know
that is not true. The first night, when I saw you in your
office, I thought you were Dorthea. But you are not.
You are beautiful and kind and good, but you are not
Dorthea. You have nothing to do with this—"

"You're wrong," Dallas heard herself saying. She didn't know where the words were coming from, but they made perfect sense to her. "There *must* be a reason why you showed up in my courtroom that night. Somehow I *am* involved. And I *want* to be involved, Miguel. I want to be your friend. I want to help you."

The commitment she heard herself making filled Dallas with a sense of awe. Also of excitement. It was a strange and unknown place she had just agreed to enter.

What had changed? What had enabled her to make that leap of faith into a world she had believed to be no more than a hallucination just a few days ago?

It was Miguel himself.

Oh, Father Kino's confirmation of Miguel's story had certainly helped. And his lack of a reflection was definitely a major contributing factor.

But the main thing was Miguel. The way she had felt in that first heartbeat when he'd materialized—and *materialized,* she understood now, was the operative word here—in her courtroom. The instantaneous recognition—*I know you. I've always known you*—that her rational mind had immediately rejected, but which still remained.

I don't want to hurt you again, he had said that first night. *When did you hurt me before?* she had asked. The question seemed like someone else's words voiced through her mouth. Dallas knew he could never have hurt her, because she had never set eyes on him in her life.

But something had hovered around the edges of her memory, just beyond her ability to recall. It suggested that he once—only once, and a very long time ago—had caused her pain so great that she'd wanted to die from it.

It was someone else's memory, but it was her own head; and it was someone else's pain, but she felt it, so deep that it was still sharp and raw in her own mind.

She shivered. Whatever that pain had been, she knew it was something she never wanted to experience firsthand.

Impulsively, she walked to the door where Miguel stood and placed her hands on his. Even before she touched him, she knew what his body would feel like. He felt warm and solid and as real as any man.

But more than that, she knew his contours, the way his skin would feel beneath her hands, the way his arms and shoulders and the long, hard muscles of his back would feel if she were to move her hands over them.

She knew how his lips would taste, and then she *did* taste them, as they covered hers with a tenderness that made her feel . . . *cherished.*

Then *cherished* became something else. Miguel unfolded his arms and took her hands in his, clasping them tightly against his chest. He deepened the kiss, and Dallas strained upward to meet his suddenly demanding mouth. Her body arched against him, and with an involuntary moan, she felt her lips part of their own volition to allow him to enter.

Cherish became stronger, more insistent. It became something urgent, something not to be denied. Was he kissing Dorthea or herself? Dallas wondered for a brief, illogical instant.

In the next instant she knew it was a question that begged the asking. In the way of genes that had been passed down through the generations, or possibly in a way more mystical than that, Dorthea was part of her and she was part of Dorthea. The thought pleased her.

"Thank you for...that," Miguel breathed huskily. He lifted his lips from hers, but his mouth was so close that the words became part of Dallas's own breath. "For you...your friendship. I knew you were kind and good, and I believe I am going to need a kind and good friend very badly before this thing is over."

"Over?" Dallas looked up, surprised. That this might be a temporary situation was something that had not occurred to her. "Why should it be over?"

Miguel tightened her hands against his chest. "I do not belong here, Dallas. Maybe it is some kind of mistake on God's part. Maybe it's a trick of the Devil's. I don't know how long I will be allowed to stay, or if I will be allowed to stay at all."

"We'll figure this out," Dallas promised. Her voice was fierce, as were her blue eyes as they fixed on his velvet brown ones. "As soon as I can clear a day, we'll drive up to Phoenix and visit the Heard Museum. Father Kino said they have the old Mission records up there, and also journals an old priest kept—"

"Father Sebastiani?" Miguel asked eagerly. Finally, he thought, something he recognized! A root, however slight, that connected him to his past.

"Yes. Father Sebastiani. Maybe you'll see something in his journals that might be important."

Dallas sounded so positive that, for the first time, Miguel felt less like a leaf adrift on some maverick wind of time. For the first time he felt that there might be something he could do to help himself. For the first time, he felt some measure of control.

But then he lowered his mouth to hers again, to her lips that were so much like Dorthea's that it seemed the most natural thing in the world to kiss them. Unwittingly, his eyes strayed to the mirror on the dresser, except for the bed, the only piece of furniture in the tiny room.

And in the mirror he saw Dallas. Her reflection was slightly off balance, leaning as she appeared to be against thin air. The palms of her hands were resting against thin air. And her lovely face was tilted upward, her lips pressed against thin air.

DECEMBER 16, Dallas thought to herself. Only eight days left until Christmas Eve.

Christmas, she figured, had to be the key.

Miguel had been murdered on Christmas Eve, and Christmas Eve was only eight days away. It made sense, if any of this could be said to make sense, that December twenty-fourth was a deadline of some sort

He had been hung on December 24, 1894. Could there be something he was supposed to do before this particular December twenty-fourth that would prevent his death one hundred years ago?

Or possibly to prevent his dying *again* in 1994? She shuddered at the horrible thought, wondering where it had come from.

The murder had taken place the day before he and Dorthea had planned to marry. Could *that* be the psychic connection between herself and him—?

"Ms. McAllister! Ms. McAllister, you seem to be woolgathering! My client's freedom is at stake here— I would appreciate your undivided attention!"

"Yes, Mr. Slocum," Dallas replied guiltily, returning her mind to the business at hand.

Devers Slocum, brother of Wyatt, had been Dallas's opposition both times she had run for justice of the peace. He was one-half of the only law firm in town, which was why he was currently before her court defending a large, unhealthy-looking de Pima woman on the charge of soliciting. Money, Dallas thought cynically, seemed to cross all boundaries.

"My client cannot afford the fifty-dollar fine you have imposed on her—"

"If your client can't afford the fine, Mr. Slocum, how is it that she can afford to hire you?"

Devers Slocum leaned closer. "She's making payments," he confided to Dallas's ear only.

More loudly, he continued. "And being a working woman, neither can she serve the three days confinement to Los Reales City Jail that is the only alternative you offered her."

"*Working woman,* Mr. Slocum?" Dallas repeated, arching one eyebrow skeptically. "Very well, what do you propose?"

"We propose dismissal of all charges—"

Upon seeing Dallas's eyes narrow dangerously, Devers Slocum immediately switched to Plan B. "She could make payments," he suggested.

As usual on Fridays, Dallas's day was full.

She always tried to clear her docket before the weekend onslaught of the Saturday Night Knife and Gun Club. Often she could accomplish this only by doubling up on her workload, making Friday an exceptionally long day.

Most of the time she enjoyed her job, and appreciated the fact that she was having a positive effect on people's lives.

She made regular visits to both elementary schools to discuss Officer Friendly, the Just Say No To Drugs program, and the respect due to school crossing guards.

She also visited the high school, speaking a bit more frankly on the legal ramification of drug use, driving under the influence, and destroying the protected desert wilderness areas with ATV's.

Today, however, the long Friday dragged on interminably. *What are all these people doing here?* she grumbled to herself as the day wore on. *Why aren't they all out Christmas shopping, like they're sup-posed to be!*

Today, she didn't feel like an officer of the court. Today, all she could think about was tomorrow.

Chapter Seven

As distances go in the desert, Miguel knew that Phoenix was not far from Los Reales—a three-day ride by horseback, maybe five days as a man could walk.

But the three-hour drive in Dallas's truck astonished him.

When the outskirts of the sprawling city came into view, she looked across the front seat with a smile. "What do you think?" she asked.

The bewildered expression that had been on Miguel's face when he'd first appeared in Dallas's courtroom was there again. As far as he was concerned, these past three hours might as well have taken him to the moon.

The Tucson Valley was in the lower part of the Sonoran Desert, a deep basin surrounded by high mountains; but the land around Phoenix was very flat. The desert stretched out in every direction as far as the eye could see, and what those who lived here called "mountains" were no more than rocky hills.

The desert was the same. The saguaro forest was still there—the giant, man-limbed cactus covered the desert floor and marched up the foothills like soldiers. There were creosote bushes and smoke trees, palo verde and the flesh-shredding cholla.

But Phoenix was no longer the city he had known.

It had been a dirty, bustling overpopulated place in the days when Miguel drove The McAllister's cattle here, to be loaded onto trains heading east. It always gave Miguel a headache to spend time in Phoenix, and it was dangerous, as well, for an Indian alone. He was always eager to get back to the Tucson Valley.

Now there was grass everywhere, and it was brighter green than desert scrub ever got, even in the summer rainy season. Trees and saguaros grew directly out of the sidewalks, and everywhere he looked he saw tall palms.

"I knew Phoenix before," he said incredulously. "It was a jump-off for those headed to the gold fields and down to Mexico. It was big then, but already I have seen more people than I ever saw in my life before. Why have they come here? Where are they going?"

Dallas smiled wryly. "I'm sure if you asked them, most wouldn't know the answers to those questions any more than you do. I lived here for a while. After a few years, I didn't know, either. So I went home."

While Dallas threaded her way through the bumper-to-bumper traffic, Miguel watched the city go by—the confusion of signs; the colorful, flashing lights that didn't appear to be lighted by gas or candles but looked like they were; the stores and shops with windows full of things he didn't recognize.

He saw tall buildings that scraped the sky. Churches, he guessed. The tallest building Miguel had ever seen in his life before now was San Xavier del Bac, and it was dwarfed by these.

Man was always trying to get closer to God, Father Sebastiani had once said. That was the reason the Indians went to the mountaintops to pray, and why churches were the tallest structures men built.

The people who lived in Phoenix had gotten closer to God for sure, but the churches they had built were so plain and gray, he wondered whether He liked having them touch His heavens.

High overhead, he saw huge and beautiful birds that flew higher than hawks; their wings were silver and reflected the sun like glass.

Everywhere there were people. So many that Miguel felt smothered, as if there were not enough air for him to breathe. And everywhere there was noise—harsh, ugly, disturbing noise.

"Do all these people live here?" he asked.

"There are over two-and-a-half-million people in Phoenix," Dallas replied. "These are only a few of them."

"How can there be enough water in the desert for so many people?"

"We don't depend on wells anymore. Now we have huge dams on rivers up north, and they channel the water where it's needed."

"A miracle." Miguel's voice was reverent. "I would like to see such a thing."

"No more a miracle than you are," Dallas pointed out with a smile.

The streets became narrower, the buildings closer, the crowds denser. The air was thick and rank, and Miguel found it hard to breathe. The chaos of the city filled him with distaste. He was quiet for a time.

"This is not a good way for people to live," he finally said with absolute conviction.

Many twists and turns later, Dallas stopped her truck in a large, open space filled with a whole herd of trucks like hers and the other smaller wagons she called "cars," all standing in lines like horses at a hitching post.

They entered a white building where it was blessedly quiet, and where the air, Miguel was amazed to discover, was as cool as an underground cave and easy to breathe.

An enclosed platform like those used in the copper mines to hoist ore, only clean and shiny, lifted them up to the second floor.

Dallas spoke to a man who sat in the middle of a large, semicircular desk. "I'd like to take a look at the records from the San Xavier Mission, please," she said.

The man's fingers clicked rapidly over the surface of his desk, then he peered into a white box that sat in front of him. "They're in the Southwest Room." He gestured left. "The librarian there can show you how to operate the microfiche viewer."

"I'd like to see the originals in the archives, please."

"I'm sorry, the originals are not available to the general public except by special permission."

Dallas produced her wallet and flashed her County Employee Identification card. "I'm a Pima County judge," she exaggerated slightly. "And this is Mr. Miguel de Pima. Mr. de Pima is a Papago...uh, historian, working on...uh, genealogical research for the tribal council."

"Do you have a notarized request from the tribal chairman?"

"Not exactly, but..." She leaned closer and smiled coaxingly. "In a way, those records *belong* to Mr. de Pima, would you think?"

The man was unmoved. "*I* might think so, ma'am," he said with bureaucratic haughtiness, "but the state of Arizona doesn't happen to agree. You'd still need a notarized request form from the tribal chairman, and then you'd need a notarized permission form from a judge."

The man flicked his fingers lightly over his desk again and studied the box in front of him; it made a couple of tiny, insect sounds. "But no matter. Since you're a *justice of the peace*—" he eyed her reprovingly "—just sign this permission form and I'll notarize it. Ms. Malone in the Southwest Room will take you to the vault."

WHEN MS. MALONE delivered the stack of age-worn journals to the library table where he and Dallas sat, Miguel felt a deep sadness overtake him.

How often had he seen these very diaries when they were new? How often had he touched their smooth leather bindings, fetching them for Father Sebastiani or placing them back on the shelf?

He opened one journal at random. The ink, once black, had faded to purple. The cramped, spidery handwriting was achingly familiar. Miguel ran his fingers over the yellowed pages, and felt almost as though he was touching the old priest.

How often had he watched Father Sebastiani bent over his desk, carefully recording in these journals the business of the Mission, the life of the tribe? In this silent room, Miguel could almost hear the scratching of the quill pen Father Sebastiani had always used, could almost hear the in and out of his breath.

"I think I've found it," Dallas announced after reading and putting aside a good many of the journals. "Listen to this," she said, "'the night of the Christ Child's birth...1894...snow...no one alive remembered such snow...'"

She turned the book sideways so that she and Miguel could read it together.

"'The McAllister's heathen posse rode their horses through the portal into the church... The McAllister's demon stallion that dared to desecrate the very altar itself with its unholy, demon hooves... The

McAllister's whip... The McAllister's daughter... The McAllister's men ... The McAllister's law....'"

If there had been any shred of doubt in Dallas's mind, any last, lingering hope that a logical explanation might still be found, the journals had banished it. Not only was Miguel's fantastical story true, but all of it—all of it—had been brought to pass by the founding father of the McAllister Clan, the righteous and honorable Judge McAllister.

"The man was a monster," Dallas moaned. Trying to comprehend all she had just read was the most difficult thing she had ever done in her life. She felt an almost irresistible compulsion to apologize to Miguel for being related to a creature as inhuman as The McAllister. Propping her elbows on the library table, she hid her face in her hands, overcome by shame.

Miguel read on. In words as brutal and pitiless as the act they described, Father Sebastiani told of that terrible night.

Again Miguel felt the terror of his hands being tied behind his back, of not even being allowed the dignity of riding like a man to his death, but instead being heaved like a sack of meal into a saddle.

Again he saw the gnarled mesquite above his head, again felt the noose around his neck. And again he heard the shot from The McAllister's rifle, felt the horse between his knees bolt, and after that the searing, red nothingness.

Now, in the time-worn journals, he finally learned what had come after that.

In the priest's own words, Miguel learned for the first time about Father Sebastiani's prophecy that God would turn His face away from the town until the desecration of His sanctuary was avenged, and the hanging of an innocent man forgiven.

To Miguel, the words didn't sound at all like kind Father Sebastiani. He had been a mild and jovial man. In the journal, even he had written that he never would have dared to speak for his Lord God in such a manner.

His own words had terrified him, the old priest said, as had his own voice, foreboding and ominous, echoing like distant thunder through the snow-covered mountains that rimmed the Tucson Valley.

Father Sebastiani's memoirs also included what had happened to The McAllister's beautiful, redheaded daughter. She had taken pneumonia after that terrible night in the snow, and had nearly died of it. When she'd recovered, months later, she seldom smiled, and never laughed. The McAllister had married her to another cattleman, a distant cousin, thereby doubling McAllister landholdings.

Miguel and Dallas looked at each other.

"What do you make of it?" Dallas whispered.

"Revenge and forgiveness. That part is plain enough. But how? And who?"

"Could it be that you're supposed to avenge your own murder somehow?" Dallas theorized.

Miguel looked doubtful. "But no," he said solemnly, "it says it is to be *forgiven*."

"You're right. Anyway the *vengeance* seems to have been exacted. Compared to the other towns in the Tucson Valley, Los Reales has certainly been left behind in the dust."

Miguel considered the possibility. "The feud!" he exclaimed. Several researchers in other parts of the room looked up disapprovingly. "Maybe that is the purpose of the feud. You said it goes back so far that no one remembers how it started. But there was no feud in my time, so it must have started *after* my—"

He lowered his voice, suddenly conscious of how the words "death" or "murder" or "hanging" would sound to someone overhearing them. *"After,"* he amended simply. "So maybe—"

"So maybe that's how it started," Dallas interrupted. Her voice sounded excited. "It makes sense."

"Yes. But why have I been sent back? What is it that *I* am supposed to do?"

"I don't know. But you pointed out the hanging has to be forgiven. You were the one who was wronged— who else would have the right to forgive except you?"

Miguel shook his head sadly. "If that is what has to be done, then I am afraid it will never be done. I cannot forgive them. I *will* not! They took away everything that was precious to me. They murdered me, Dallas. How can I be expected to forgive that?"

"I don't know," she repeated unhappily.

"I could *say* I have forgiven them," Miguel went on in a hard, deliberate voice, as if to keep it from exploding into a howl of outrage. "I could even try to believe it. But deep in my heart, I would know it was not true. And God would know. Only He could forgive such a mortal sin.''

LEAVING THE MUSEUM, they were surprised to find that it had grown dark outside. But not really dark, for the glow from the city lights of Phoenix turned the night sky to gray and faded the stars so that only the brightest could be seen.

When they walked to the truck in the nearly empty parking lot and climbed inside, Dallas consulted her watch by the light of the dashboard. ''Nearly nine o'clock,'' she said, dismayed. ''I'd expected to be back in Los Reales by now!''

''Why?''

''Oh, just the way the town is, I guess. It'd be a lot easier not to attract attention earlier in the day, when people are busy with other things. But at midnight, which is about when we'll get back, everyone'll be checking out a strange set of headlights on their street. Saturday night gets pretty wild in Los Reales.''

''Saturday night was like that in my time, too,'' Miguel said with his slow, grave smile.

Dallas headed toward Interstate 10 that led to Tucson, but not more than half an hour out of Phoenix, she found that the deserted highway with its monotonous white lines was having a hypnotic effect on her.

She rolled down the window to let the cold air rush in on her face. When that didn't help, she prudently pulled over to the shoulder of the highway. Resting her head against the back of the seat, she took several deep breaths.

"You are tired," Miguel said. "It has been a long day for you."

"No, not really." Then Dallas laughed. "I haven't had a good night's sleep since the day—the night—I met you."

"Why is that?"

"Well, gee," she replied. "First I was afraid *for* you, afraid you'd go wandering around some part of town where you shouldn't and some crazy McAllister would take after you. Then I was afraid *of* you. And now...now..."

"Now?"

Her voice fell. "Now I'm afraid you won't find out your reason for being here, and you'll be taken away from me."

"I am glad to know that I am so much in your thoughts," Miguel said softly, "because you are also very much in mine."

Sliding an arm around her shoulders, he gently pulled Dallas across the seat and pressed her head to his chest. "Sleep for a little while. Let the town gossip if they will—they know nothing of what is between you and me."

Dallas snuggled briefly against him, but suddenly sleep was the farthest thing from her mind. What had begun only five days ago as a strange encounter had suddenly taken on all the passion of the reunion of long-lost lovers.

Emotions she had come to believe were lacking in her nature overwhelmed her now with an urgency that shocked her. Her only cogent thought was that she wanted this man with a ferocity she had never felt before in her life. She *needed* him, something inside her cried out, and she knew that she had needed him for a very long time.

She had known a lot of men in her life, including some she had known *all* of her life. Some were attractive, some were charming, exciting, and fun to be with. A few eventually became her very good friends.

But none had ever done more than scratch the surface of her emotions. None had been the sort of man with whom she was willing to share her body or her life. None had brought forth the kind of response Miguel had since the very first time he had taken her in his arms and asked if tomorrow was still their wedding day. Nor had any created the feelings he was arousing now, simply by holding her in his arms and stroking her cheek as though he were coaxing a child to sleep.

She looked up at him through the shadows of her lashes.

"Aren't you tired, too?" she asked, wondering if he could hear the need in her voice.

"Sh-h-h, do not worry about me. I will nap awhile later on." He continued to caress her cheek.

"Yes, but...you've had a long day, too. And you've got a lot to think about. Maybe you should start out tomorrow fresh, not all kinked up from trying to sleep in a truck. Maybe we should stop for the night at a...a motel.''

"What is that?"

"It's a hotel, sort of, for people who're driving and get tired and need to sleep for a while. Like us. Then we can get on the road early in the morning, and maybe sneak back into town while everyone is sleeping late or in church."

She wondered if he would understand the implications of her suggestion. He didn't appear to, and she felt guilty, almost as though she were trying to seduce him.

Was she?

It was true that she was tired.

It was also true that she hadn't had a good night's sleep in a week.

And it was certainly true that it would be easier to slip unnoticed into town on a peaceful Sunday morning than on a brawling Saturday night.

Still, she suspected, those were rationalizations. She knew her pulse wouldn't be quickening the way it was over the prospect of a good night's sleep.

"Where would we find such a place?" Miguel asked.

Dallas straightened and slid across the seat to the driver's side.

"We're only a few miles outside Gila Bend," she said in a voice she struggled, and failed, to keep matter-of-fact. "I'm sure we'll find one there."

One room or two? was the question that occupied her mind all the way into Gila Bend. One room? Or two?

Two, she finally decided. Regretfully.

Then why are ye stoppin' at all? whispered a mocking voice inside her head—a lilting, feminine voice that had, oddly enough, the faintest suggestion of brogue.

Dallas found herself saved from having to make a decision by the yawning desk clerk who answered the night bell. "One room, two double beds. It's all I got. Take it or leave it."

WHEN THEY STEPPED inside the motel room and closed the door behind them, Miguel looked around with surprise. "There are no other travelers? We are to stay together in this room?" he asked.

"Well . . . yes," Dallas replied. "There are separate beds, after all, and it's only for one night."

Miguel shook his head. "Two beds make no difference," he insisted. "We cannot stay alone together. You would be dishonored."

He turned as if to go. "I will sleep in the truck."

"Miguel, wait. Listen. Didn't you ever spend any time alone with Dorthea?"

"Of course. The time we spent with each other was always alone—there was no other way."

"Well, did that dishonor her?"

"The McAllister thought so. But it was not true," Miguel replied with simple dignity.

"The McAllister isn't here," Dallas pointed out. "And it's a different world now between men and women. We can do as we like, and no one judges us except ourselves."

How easily she says that, Miguel marveled; as if it were the most natural thing in the world. He wondered if things had really changed so much in one hundred years? Were men somehow tamer now? That was difficult to believe.

For himself, he knew the extraordinary amount of self-control it was requiring of him to keep himself from catching Dallas in his arms and kissing her until she had no will left.

But kissing would not be enough. Holding would not be enough. He knew that if his passion broke free, he would not stop until he had all of her, had her stretched out beneath him, had her in all the secret, unmentionable ways a man wants a woman.

Dallas was right about one thing, though. If he allowed himself to do as he liked, he would be his own harshest judge. He had made a vow not to hurt her again, and he would not!

Inwardly, Miguel groaned. The fire that had flashed to life the first moment he had set eyes on her from the far end of her courtroom was consuming him now. He turned away, not wanting Dallas to see the rising evidence of his need.

He groaned again, this time, against his will, almost audibly. It was going to be a very long night.

DALLAS WATCHED his broad back, the straight black hair that grew past his shoulders, the muscles that rippled in those shoulders when he moved, then narrowed down to a vee where his shirt was tucked into his trousers.

She was ashamed of herself. The man was caught in the middle of a mystery of cosmic proportions, and all she could think of was being naked with him, touching him, being touched, feeling him move inside her.

How can you be so callous? her conscience berated her.

A few abject adjectives later, she spoke in the direction of Miguel's back. "It was probably a bad idea to stop," she said by way of apology. "But since we're here, let's just go to bed—*sleep,*" she amended quickly. "We need to get an early start tomorrow."

She took off her boots and padded in her stocking feet to the bathroom, where she refreshed herself as best she could, then returned to the room and slipped fully dressed between the sheets of the nearest bed.

Having removed his own boots, Miguel sat on the edge of the other bed, his hands propped on his knees. "You make it very difficult for a man," he growled, scowling. "Do you know that?"

"I don't mean to," Dallas replied.

I meant to make it easy, she thought ruefully, mocking herself.

She felt humble. If it'd been any man but Miguel, she'd probably be lying alone in her bed right now, filled with remorse, while he snored away to beat the band on the other bed. That was the motel experience, as she had always heard it.

"I guess sometimes I forget that we're from two different worlds," she added. "Literally."

She stacked her pillows against the headboard, then punched a depression in the middle and leaned back into them. "It's just that, since we read Father Sebastiani's journals, I've had the strangest feeling..."

Miguel stood and crossed the two feet of carpet that separated them. "What feeling?" he said, hitching one hip onto the edge of Dallas's bed so that he faced her.

"That we should...be together," she whispered, with that now familiar feeling that someone else was putting words into her mouth. "That *we* waited too long the last time. That *we* can't let it happen this time."

"I pray it will not. But I said I would not hurt you again, and I will not. I will not have you made a part of all this. It has nothing to do with you—"

"But it does, Miguel, don't you see? I'm a direct descendant of the man who killed you and I can't shake the feeling that I am somehow bonded to Dorthea, as well. I *am* a part of this."

"Dorthea did nothing wrong, except to love me. She was a victim. I will not make you a victim, too. I don't know if I will be allowed to stay in your world, but I *will* not break the heart of another beautiful redhaired woman and ruin her life."

Smiling the slow, somber smile that never seemed to reach his eyes, he moved the tips of his fingers as lightly as a kiss across her lips. "I will not love you, Dallas, and I will not let you love me."

Then he stood. "Go to sleep now. Don't forget we want to slip into town while everyone is asleep."

Chapter Eight

"Only six days before Christmas," proclaimed a coy, seductive voice on the morning radio. "Don't know what to get your own special Christmas angel? How about a gift certificate for an intimate candlelit dinner for two at Beef on the Hoof—fine steaks, personally selected for you by our in-house butcher, then mesquite-grilled precisely to your order. Afterward, 'hoof' around the largest dance floor in the Southwest to the strains of the Manny Roper Quartet, playing all of your favori—"

Dallas's hand shot out from beneath the blankets and took a swipe at the clock radio. She yawned and stretched, and sleepily rolled over to find Miguel sitting upright in the middle of his bed.

"I heard a voice!" he exclaimed, glaring suspiciously around the room.

Dallas yawned and stretched again, then smiled reassuringly as she swung her legs over the edge of the bed.

"It was only an alarm clock," she told him. "A talking alarm clock, I guess you could call it. And that advertisement just reminded me—we didn't even have supper last night. I'm starving. How about you?"

BREAKFAST OPTIONS along this deserted stretch of the interstate between Gila Bend and Tucson were limited. Dallas swerved into the very next roadside café with its lights on.

Over fried eggs and hash browns, bacon and biscuits, and refills of coffee from a bottomless pot, she tried to rationalize her behavior of the previous night.

She'd been running on instinct. After a day spent in another world, walking around in the mind and the memories of an old priest long dead, she felt dazed and confused. Her reality had been turned upside down. It was one thing to consider intellectually the possibility of reincarnations; it was quite another to be confronted by it in black and white—or in this case, in purple ink and aged, yellowed paper.

She'd been frightened. Her foundations had been shaky, and she'd felt the need to anchor herself in her own world. She felt the need to anchor Miguel, as well, for fear he'd vanish back into that unknown, supernatural limbo between life and death. Making love had seemed the answer. What could be earthier, more life-affirming?

Of course, she admitted more honestly to herself, there was no getting around the fact that, quite simply, she wanted him to make love to her. Rationalize though she might, it simply came down to that.

Last night, in the dark intimacy of the truck, with the dash lights glowing and the radio playing softly, Los Reales and its problems had seemed very far away. The only thing that mattered to Dallas was him, and her, and the irresistible desire to reach across the scant two feet of leather that separated them.

This morning, after she had as much as invited Miguel into her bed last night and he had refused, she'd expected to feel foolish. Humiliated. Rejected. Instead she felt . . . cherished. He had refused her because he didn't want to hurt her—how could that be bad?

Today, of course, she was glad. Glad he'd had more self-control than she did. Glad he'd had more sense. Making love would have been nothing more than a temporary escape; surely there were certainly things more pressing in their lives.

Still, she couldn't help studying him across the booth, wondering somewhere in the back of her mind what it would have been like if he hadn't been so . . . *honorable*, in his strict definition of the word.

His dark eyes were a bit heavy-lidded, as though he, too, had had a restless night. His black hair, long and straight, looked like something out of an old cowboy-and-Indian movie. Ditto for the bandanna he wore around it.

The clothes Father Kino had given him were obviously meant for a heavier man. A well-worn sheepskin jacket hung shapelessly on his shoulders. The washed-thin chambray shirt was tucked loosely into jeans that had come by their faded look honestly, the two held together with a leather belt cinched tightly around his waist.

But he was, nevertheless, extremely attractive. Outfit him with a fashionable haircut, Dallas thought, and tight jeans, a custom-fitted Western shirt, and a new pair of Justin Ropers, then sit him on a bar stool on Saturday night and he'd look as contemporary as every other good-looking drugstore cowboy trying to score.

The image repelled her.

She liked him better like this. In Father Kino's old clothes, he looked . . . real. The bones of his face were sharp and strong, his brows were straight and black, and his dark eyes were permanently narrowed, like a man who spent much of his time working in the sun. His mouth was a straight line, too, usually solemn and unsmiling—except now, when he was making quick work of the plain home cooking on his plate.

She liked watching him eat. He did it enthusiastically, as if he hadn't seen food for a very long time— *Stop!* she ordered herself firmly.

Still, he *did* look as though he belonged to an earlier time, when food was simpler, when people were simpler, when life was simpler.

She liked that, too.

BREAKFAST FINISHED, they returned to the truck and continued on their way.

Back in Los Reales, Dallas circled around and drove into town from the south, dropping Miguel off at the Quitos' small parcel of land.

"What are you going to do now?" she asked as he slid out of the truck.

"Live," he said simply.

"But... but *how?*"

Miguel gave her a grave smile and a slight shrug of his shoulders. "The only way I can. With hard work and patience, and faith that the way will be shown to me. What else can I do?"

Dallas stalled, reluctant to leave. "Will you call me?"

"Yes." Miguel had in his pocket the card she had given him, a card with her telephone number on it. A truly amazing thing, this telephone. Just about everyone in town had one, she'd told him.

Once, in Tucson all those years ago, Miguel had seen some men demonstrating this new invention, but it had seemed something of no practical purpose. What need could there possibly be to telephone someone in the next room, as the men who demonstrated it had done? He had never believed it would catch on, much less ever reach as far as a remote desert town like Los Reales.

MIGUEL HUNKERED DOWN between the graves. He chopped away at the tenacious cat's claw that crept between the irregularly placed mounds and grew in clumps of dark green over the headstones. Often, in raking the vines away from the carved headstones, he came across a name that he recognized.

Beneath the growing vines were the thick, woody stems of their ancestor vines, possibly the very same that Miguel, as a child, had chopped and pulled for Father Sebastiani.

It was a more difficult task now, for the vines had been left to grow wild in the old Indian burial ground for longer than Father Kino could remember. Years, the priest had guessed.

Miguel stood and stretched his back. The work was hard, and the afternoon sun was hot, even in these cool winter days.

Beyond the cemetery, he looked out across fields that had once been garden tended by his people. What had been made green and fertile by their irrigation ditches and hand-carried water had now been reclaimed by the desert.

He propped his palms on top of the rake handle, rested his chin on the backs of his hands, and stared out across the ruined fields. So many changes, he mused; many of them good, but some very sad.

He longed for a sign, something that would tell him what was expected of him.

This feud between the McAllisters and the de Pimas and their like had been going on so long that it had invaded like poisoned groundwater every part of life in Los Reales. What could a single man, and a stranger at that, hope to accomplish in a few short weeks?

Miguel believed, as Dallas did, that since Christmas Eve marked the one hundred year anniversary of his hanging, it had to be a deadline, a turning point of some sort.

Even if the feud had begun over his own death, what did that have to do with him? He hadn't asked to be a martyr; he hadn't asked that his life end beneath a hanging tree. And he certainly hadn't asked for a feud to be started in his name! And he certainly couldn't be expected to forgive the men who'd murdered him.

He was just an ordinary man. He had tried to live his life according to the laws of his people and of Father Sebastiani, and of the white government that was taking over the territory.

The only mistake he'd made was falling in love with Dorthea McAllister.

And how could his love for Dorthea have been a mistake when God Himself had taken his dearest Paio, when God Himself had required Miguel to go out and find work among the whites, when God Himself had placed a beautiful, red-haired angel in his path that day of the round-up at The McAllister's ranch?

For the many months he had worked for The McAllister, the wealthiest cattleman in the territory, Miguel had been a range hand. He'd slept out under the stars for weeks at a time, seeing no one but

Cookie, and the several other cowboys who rode the same section.

Although the others had gone into town occasionally—Ajo or Marana, or Los Reales—Miguel, being Indian, could not. Did not dare. But the pay had been regular, and he'd been able to send a good portion of it back to Paio's family at Indian Oasis.

At the roundup that first spring, his section had rounded up their rangy cattle and the spring crop of calves and driven them to Los Reales—the former to be loaded onto trains bound for Kansas City, the latter to be branded with The McAllister's distinctive three-bar A.

It had been a busy and lively time, almost like a fiesta. Everyone on the ranch took part.

Even The McAllister's tight-lipped, sour-faced wife, and his gay, red-haired daughter had been in the thick of it; keeping beans cooking in a huge kettle over a campfire, roasting ears of corn, and pumping great quantities of water from one of The McAllister's many private wells.

Miguel had noticed the daughter, Dorthea, first because of her red hair, hair the like of which he had never seen before. Not restrained in a tight little bun at the nape of her neck like her mother's, it sprang wild and free down her shoulders. Each individual strand appeared to have a life of its own, flying in its own separate direction.

The first time he'd seen her, it had been dusk. He'd been herding cattle all day, and was dirty and tired and thirsty.

Smiling, she'd handed up to him a dipperful of water, and he had emptied it like an animal, splashing much of it down his chin and neck, splashing some on her, as well. He'd felt like the unworthiest of men, but she'd only laughed, and a ray of the setting sun had flashed behind her, turning her hair to flame.

Later he'd noticed her strong arms, pumping water from the well, hanging the heavy kettle over the fire, and lifting it off. Miguel had never realized that women had muscles the way men did—the women of the Papago, though hardworking, had bodies short and made round by layers of soft, female flesh.

After that he'd noticed her all the time, although never too obviously and never too close. She'd caught the notice of all the cowboys who'd worked the roundup, and The McAllister had kept his eyes on all of them. He'd been ready to brand with his own three-bar A *any* man who dawdled too long over his plate of beans, or drank too long at the well.

It was at the second roundup, the following spring, that Miguel had lost his heart to her.

That year, The McAllister had been down with the gout, and couldn't keep such a watchful eye on his ranch hands.

His sons had inherited the responsibility for Dorthea. But they, glad to be out from under their father's thumb, had spent as much time as possible away from the roundup, in the saloons.

That year, Dorthea had matured, and was more beautiful than ever. She'd remembered Miguel from the previous spring, and she'd asked how his year had been, how he'd liked being a cowboy, and how he'd liked working for her father.

She'd asked about his life at the Mission, and he had found himself telling her about the flight of his people to Indian Oasis. He had told her about Paio and the boy. He'd been so lonely that he had told her everything, and she had cried, and in that way she had become part of his life.

"Nice job, Miguel," Father Kino's voice interrupted his thoughts.

Wearing a straw sombrero, the priest was seated in his truck—a red, four-wheel-drive Subaru station wagon, he had informed Miguel proudly, which could climb over the steepest cliffs like a mountain goat. Miguel found it hard to give the lie to a priest, but he *did* find that story a difficult one to swallow.

Father Kino leaned out the window of his Subaru. "Sunday afternoon is my favorite time of the week," he said cheerfully to Miguel. "The week's work is done, and the new week's work hasn't begun yet."

"Speaking of work—" he glanced appreciatively around the old cemetery with its irregularly spaced graves and low adobe wall "—I've never seen the place look so fine. It's a shame to let it get so overgrown, isn't it? But there doesn't seem to be anyone to tend it. You can see from the headstones how old it is—there's probably no one left alive who remembers these folks.''

"*I* remember them. My mother and father—''

At Father Kino's sudden, sharp look, he stopped short, but his mind continued the litany of old friends and old relatives buried here. *My uncle Ono'ham. Cruzo, my neighbor and Cruzo's woman, who outlived him by over half a lifetime according to the dates on her headstone. Ahil, my old friend. And, of course, Paio.*

But he found no grave marker for the boy. Perhaps he had never returned. Perhaps he had died at Indian Oasis. Perhaps farther away than that, or among strangers, where no one knew what village he'd come from.

It brought slow tears to Miguel's eyes to recall the small, solemn-eyed child. He hoped that he had lived a long life, and that he slept now among friends.

Miguel found no grave marker with his own name carved into it, either. They had not given him a Christian burial, then, he thought, not surprised. Most likely they had just scratched out a depression in the frozen ground and left him for the coyotes to find in the spring.

Is that why I am here? Miguel wondered suddenly.

Am I doomed to forever wander the earth because I have no grave in which to rest? What if there is no purpose at all to my return, except to search endlessly and fruitlessly for my own bones to put them to rest?

The thoughts chilled him.

"Yes...well, all the same," Father Kino again broke into his musings with determined joviality, "you've done a fine job. I hope you'll decide to stay around for a while. There's a great deal of work that needs to be done."

"Yes," Miguel replied slowly. "There *is* a great deal of work to be done here. It is difficult to know where to begin."

The priest's eyes narrowed sharply. "What do you mean?"

"The vines," Miguel explained. With one arm he made a sweeping gesture that included the neglected gardens behind the Mission, once tended by Indians. Now they were a matted wilderness of dark green cat's claw vines.

"They are bad in a garden," Miguel continued. "Left to themselves, they are like weeds. Once they are allowed to take root, they will take over a garden and choke the life out of it. And it is difficult to uproot them, for they send runners underground where you cannot see them, so that you never know where they will next appear."

Father Kino looked thoughtful. It occurred to him to wonder if they were talking only about cat's claw vines and gardens. "And how do you eradicate these weeds, once they've established themselves?"

"With much patience," Miguel replied. "And much hard work."

Father Kino nodded, still thoughtful. "Yes, I see," he remarked in a meditative tone. "Two traits it would behoove all of us to learn, whatever gardens we labor in."

He reached into his pocket, then extended his arm toward Miguel to place two soft and very faded twenty-dollar bills in his hand.

Miguel looked at him blankly.

"You must not let people take advantage of you," the priest admonished gently. "You're going to need money to get along, you know."

Money. Miguel took the unfamiliar green paper and stuffed it into his pocket. "Thank you, Father."

"Thank *you*, my son. Mrs. Quito has a supper ready for you in the kitchen."

With that, he gunned his engine and headed out toward the Huachuca foothills—looking, no doubt, Miguel imagined, for a mountain for his red Subaru to climb.

Chapter Nine

Just before the noon hour of a very busy Monday morning, Dallas looked up from her desk to see another apparition at the back of her courtroom.

This time it was Rooster. He was wearing his usual mad-at-the-world expression, and Dallas couldn't tell whether this was a social call or business.

Business, as it turned out.

He waited, glaring balefully at her from the back of the room, until she dispensed with the last case of the morning. Then he stumped up to her desk.

"Hi, Pa," Dallas said. "What can I do for you?"

"Heard you was up to Phoenix," he began without preamble.

"That's right." Dallas stiffened defensively. "What about it?"

"Whyn't you tell me you was goin'? I might's needed you to bring me back somethin'."

"Why, Pa? It's been a long time since I've kept you informed about my comings and goings."

"Heard you didn't go alone."

"That's nobody's business but my own."

"That so?" Her father appeared to consider that statement thoughtfully. "I don't know what makes you think that, Dorothy Alice, when the whole town knows about it. *And* knows who you want up there with. *And* knows the two of you didn't get back till the next mornin'."

"I don't care what everyone thinks they know, Pa!" Dallas exclaimed heatedly. She jumped to her feet, nearly overturning the desk chair as she shoved it backward. "This is my life, and I'll do with it what I choose!"

"That'd be a real mistake, girl. Even though you *are* a McAllister, you can't go around spittin' in the face of the whole town and expect to gets away with it. This bastid you're runnin' around with is a *de Pima,* for God's sake! What for you want to go ruinin' your reputation for a goddamn *de Pima?*"

"What about my reputation, Pa?" Dallas said. Her voice was dangerously controlled.

She'd heard that kind of talk before; only the last time, it had come from Miguel and had sounded a great deal kinder and more caring than it did being hurled at her by old Rooster.

"They're sayin' things about you, Dorothy Alice. Calling you names. Slut, for one. Squaw, for another. And a few I'd kill a man for sayin' if I wasn't afraid he had good reason to say it."

Rooster's voice quavered for a moment, asking Dallas with its gruff but pleading tone to deny the rumors he'd heard. "I'll take your word for it, girl. Tell me it ain't true. Tell me everythin' they're all sayin' about you ain't true...."

Dallas flashed back to Miguel's words again. *I would never have dishonored Dorthea—I loved her too much. But The McAllister believed I did.* "Doesn't matter, does it, Pa? If the whole town thinks it's true, it's as good as, right?"

"Don't smart-mouth me, Dorothy Alice! Just think about it for a minute. Even if you don't care what everybody thinks, someday you're gonna wanna get married and settle down—how you gonna feel when all the young bucks in town think you're spoiled goods—"

"Spoiled goods!" Her voice rose an octave. "This town is full of spoiled goods, Pa—most of them wearing boots and Stetsons, and strutting around pretending they're somebody when they're nothing but losers!"

"Taint natural, girl, you thinking that way. And neither is running around with a bounden enemy of your own kind. Thought I raised you better'n that. If your ma'd stuck around—"

"Wouldn't have changed a thing, Pa." That might be true, but not in the way her father meant. In fact, Dallas sometimes wondered if it wasn't her mother's leaving that had made her take a long, hard look at the feud and come to the conclusion that she wanted nothing whatsoever to do with it.

Rooster propped both hands on the head of his cane and rocked backward and then forward on his heels.

Some things you might wanna keep in mind, Dorothy Alice,'' he said. "You're a McAllister, and you're my girl, and no one's gonna bother you much, even if you *are* a fool. But this de Pima, that's another story. He could be in big trouble. *Big* trouble."

He fixed Dallas with a baleful eye. "You don't wanna be ruining your name in this town over a dead man, do you?"

As was so often the case, her encounter with Rooster left Dallas fuming, and this time, frightened, as well. As a child, after a run-in with Rooster, she would often take her mare, Cassie, and race through the desert until both she and the horse were exhausted. When she would return home, hours later, she would have run the anger clean out of herself.

All grown up now, a responsible citizen with a responsible job, she couldn't deal with her anger that way anymore, especially not in the middle of a workday.

Still, it was what she longed to do—run away for a while, breathe in fresh air, clear her head of Rooster's perverse bullheadedness.

Instead of popping a frozen burrito into the microwave she kept in the back room, she suddenly decided to go out for lunch. She seized her purse, slammed out of the office, and locked the door behind her.

Most of the businesses along Main Street closed for lunch, and the dusty street was empty, the only activity being tiny tufts of sand blowing before the wind.

The cool winter sun was directly overhead, giving the desert air a warmth that would be gone by four o'clock. Almost like a ride in the desert, the fresh air cleared the anger from her head. Her furious, heel-pounding strides slowed gradually to a walk, and she found herself thinking calmly about what Rooster had said.

Pa doesn't bump his gums without good reason, she reasoned. She understood that he had come to see her today not only to rebuke her, but to warn her.

What insanity had made her think she could escape the prying eyes of Los Reales?

Although she had never cared one way or the other what the town thought, she had never crossed the invisible but inviolate line the feud had drawn in the sand, either.

Miguel could indeed be in big trouble.

CHAUNCY'S Twenty-Four-Hour Diner wasn't really open around the clock, but Chauncy thought the name sounded very upscale, as though there might really be a need for a twenty-four-hour diner in a place like Los Reales.

All the VIP's in town held court in Chauncy's around lunch time, which often lasted until the bars opened, when they adjourned to their watering holes of choice.

Most of the young bucks were there, as usual, Dallas noted as she entered through the double glass doors.

Sitting together at a single table were Wyatt Slocum, who treated her with an infuriating air of proprietorship; his brother Devers, whom she knew expected to succeed her as justice of the peace once she married Wyatt and settled down to producing a passel of kids; Tommy Lee McAllister, the very distant cousin who owned the feed store and always smelled like chemicals and fertilizer.

There was also Gil Trout, good-looking, thrice-divorced, and so habitually unpunctual with his child-support payments that he was a routine defendant before Dallas's court.

Then there was Petit Cobb, recently paroled from the state penitentiary, where he'd been serving time for shooting a man in a barroom brawl. Because the man was a de Pima, Petit was a local hero, and the townsfolk just couldn't imagine why the judge hadn't seen it that way.

Good ol' boys all, Dallas thought sourly. Sometimes she joined them at lunch, but today she only nodded curtly in their direction and walked on.

She felt the eyes of the men following her. Suddenly she understood what the trite old phrase "undressing her with their eyes" meant, and it gave her an ugly sense of vulnerability.

Feeling awkward, and feeling even more awkward because she did, Dallas slid into a solitary booth at the rear. She heard voices fall as she passed, heard someone give a single, insulting bark of a laugh.

She had grown up with these men, gone to school and Sunday school with them, and dated them in high school; when had they become predators, and she prey?

She had to admit that it wasn't just the slim pickings in Los Reales that kept her away from the altar.

The years she'd spent in Phoenix had been the same; even the nice guys were only that—nice guys. Dallas knew there was love in the world. She knew there was passion and caring beyond the pale imitations she saw all around her, but she had begun to doubt that it would ever come to her.

Until Miguel de Pima had appeared in her courtroom.

She tried to picture him in this diner, in these surroundings. She couldn't. And suddenly she realized that she couldn't picture herself here, either.

"Barbecue and fries," she said to the waitress who hovered above her, pad and pencil at the ready. "And an ice tea with lemon. To go."

FATHER KINO was worried about what was happening in Los Reales. The rumors that reached his ears were ugly and vicious. He was afraid someone was going to get hurt.

It had been a long time since any serious violence had erupted in Los Reales, the last time being when a mining company had tried to reopen the copper mine at Wood Rat Wells.

The de Pima and McAllister contingents of aspiring miners had fought tooth and nail to keep the other side out, and the whole bloody mess had culminated in Petit Cobb's shooting of Raoul de Pima outside a south-side bar.

The mine project had gone south to Tumacacori, and with it, the hundred-plus jobs Los Reales had sorely needed.

At sundown, on his knees before the altar of the Mission church, Father Kino decided to offer his vespers prayer for peace in the town.

It was, perhaps, a thankless task, to plead for Divine intercession, especially for people who hugged their hatred to their bosoms as if it were treasure, but he felt it necessary to try.

Even as he recited his vespers, however, Father Kino couldn't seem to keep his thoughts on the town, or on the feud.

Images ran through his mind, disjointed and out of focus, like a film poorly spliced.

The pretty, freckled face of Dallas McAllister was one such image; odd, because she wasn't a member of his flock. But Father Kino liked her and respected her for the fair and evenhanded way she handled her position as justice of the peace—the first McAllister ever to do so, and at great personal risk, he knew.

Miguel de Pima's image also moved through his mind. What was it about the strange young Indian, who had appeared seemingly out of nowhere, that captured the priest's imagination and held it?

Father Kino pictured him standing beside an almost man-high heap of dark green cat's claw vines, the leaves already beginning to wilt in the sun.

Patience, Miguel had advised in the matter of uprooting weeds in a garden, although, of course, the same could apply to many things. *Patience. And hard work.*

Unbidden, Father Sebastiani's journals came into his mind.

His rosary forgotten, Father Kino stared at the altar, trying to envision the violent and godless scene that had taken place there one hundred years ago.

Fear... and pain, and foreboding... horses filling the open spaces where the pews now stood... armed men. The McAllister, the personification of evil as drawn by Father Sebastiani's pen...

And a young Indian, who for some inexplicable reason, bore the face of the man who had appeared at his door a week ago... A screaming, red-haired woman... The McAllister's daughter... The desecration of God's holy altar, and a courageous priest risking his life trying to prevent it...

Would he have had the courage of that old priest? Father Kino wondered. Different things were required of priests today—the ability to make small talk at social gatherings, for example; the ability to coax money out of board members and trustees; administrative and financial skills. At bottom, were they still defenders of the faith, lions of God, as the old priests had been?

Was *he?*

Father Kino shivered. It was always cold in the church these short days of winter, he thought vaguely. The cold old walls still reverberated with the brutality of another day. The pitiless images conjured up by his imagination hung heavy in the still air.

Could it be . . . ?

Could it be . . . that Miguel de Pima really *was* the young Indian of the old legend? Had he been sent to remind him of his mission in this godforsaken town?

The history of the early church was full of such legends—was it possible that such things still happened today?

The sun had just dipped behind the horizon when Father Kino heard the voices of children singing in the distance. He remembered that Mrs. Quito had mentioned she was making *bizcochuelos* and fry bread for a *posadas* of Papago children from the reservation.

For some reason the children's voices made him think of Fred Coppersmith, pastor at the Christian Fellowship Hall on Main Street. Relieved, for the time being, to be free from pondering universal mysteries, Father Kino walked to his office and picked up the telephone.

"Hi, Fred," he said when the phone on the other end was answered. "How're the charity collections going this year? Yeah, we're down here, too. Look, Fred, have you got a *posadas* on for tonight? Well, the reason I called is—what do you think about rounding up a van and bringing your kids out here?''

In the moment of surprised silence on the other end, Father Kino's voice hurried on. "Mrs. Q.'s got homemade *bizcochuelos* for a bunch of kids from the reservation and a few southsiders who attend mass here. And knowing her, she's made twice as much as we need. I wouldn't be surprised if she's probably got a piñata hung, too.... You will? Great! You were? Well, you know what they say about great minds! Good thing you didn't call me the same time I called you, or both of us would have gotten busy signals! Just come on over after the procession, then. We'll be expecting you.''

Then he said something neither clergyman could have explained in words, but which both viscerally understood. "We don't have any more time to lose.''

Chapter Ten

Dallas stepped down to the sidewalk and locked her office door behind her.

Main Street was as deserted at seven o'clock as it had been at noon. The only difference was that now it was dark, as well.

In the distance she heard voices singing Christmas carols. It was *Las Posadas* procession. It sounded as though the voices came from Reverend Coppersmith's Christian Fellowship Hall, a storefront meeting house a little farther down Main Street.

Dallas smiled. The music of a *posadas* always reminded her of *Las Posadas* of her own childhood, and the Christmas she had played Mary in the procession, and the red-letter Christmas Eve when she had been the one to break open the piñata and let all the candy spill out.

More than decorated trees, more than Santa Claus, even more than gift-giving, taking part in *Las Posadas* was the true meaning of Christmas for the children of the Southwest.

Despite the concerns that weighed on her mind, Dallas found herself humming along with the children's song.

Approaching her truck in the public parking lot behind city hall, Dallas noticed that the streetlight under which she had parked was dark. She made a mental note to call public utilities—who knew how long it would take them to get around to replacing it on their own?

Then she noticed broken glass glittering dully on the ground around the truck, and on the hood, as well. Looking up, she saw that the light had not burned out—it had been shot out. Shooting out streetlights was not an uncommon recreational activity for vandals seeking a little after-hours' entertainment.

Suddenly a shadow loomed behind the truck, then several more, the shapes only a little darker than the night that concealed their identities. As silently as ghosts, the shadows drifted out from behind the truck and encircled it, draping themselves on the hood, on the fender, against the door.

Dallas stopped short. She heard the flick of a cigarette lighter. Once. Twice. A tiny flame illuminated for an instant a face she couldn't recognize.

Her heart began to pound.

"Hello, Judge," a voice said softly into the darkness. "Working kinda late tonight, ain't cha?"

"Ain't your Indian boyfriend gonna be wondering where you are?" said another. Softly. Dangerously.

"Please get away from my vehicle," Dallas commanded in her sternest, most authoritative tone.

"Oh, now, Judge, don't be that way," said a third voice. "We just hadn't realized you was that horny. Lots o' guys in town woulda been happy to service you—you didn't have to go off with no de Pima."

"You're a mighty-fine-lookin' woman, Judge, you don't wanna waste a body like that on an *Injun*." A fourth voice spat out the last word, along with a cud of chew.

Who were they? In the dark she couldn't see their faces. Neither did she recognize their voices, but she was sure she must know them—most of the criminal element in town had been through her court at one time or another.

"All right, now that you've all had your say, get away from my truck."

Slowly, menacingly, the shadows shifted their positions, not away from the truck, but around it to the driver's side. She heard a low, ugly laugh. An excited laugh.

The outrage she'd felt at first quickly turned to panic. The ugly, excited laugh told her the level of tension was escalating.

"Listen, fellas, you're in a lot of trouble here. You don't threaten a law officer. Now get away and let me by."

"Sure, Judge, anything you want."

The shadows parted, leaving a narrow aisle between them that Dallas had no inclination in the world to cross. Instead she fell back a step.

"I don't think the lady knows what she wants," said one voice sneeringly.

"Me, neither," replied another. "Not when she's running around with a de Pima, she don't."

"Maybe she just don't know what a real man is."

"We could show her. Would you like that, Judge?" It was the soft, suggestive voice that had first spoken. The hand holding the cigarette threw it to the ground, and the shadow advanced languidly, arrogantly, toward her.

"Get away from me," Dallas cried, and swung at him viciously with her briefcase.

It was a mistake, she realized that the instant she did it. With the hostile gesture, she had let them know she was afraid, and she had escalated the level of violence. Again she heard the soft, ugly laugh. It sounded more menacing than before, and it was coming closer.

Suddenly light flooded the parking lot. Whirling around, Dallas was immediately blinded by the headlights of a car.

"Ms. McAllister, that you? What's going on here?" Dallas recognized the voice of one of Los Reales's finest. She heard the crunch of gravel under booted feet as the four shadows took on human form and fled across the parking lot.

The deputy pursued them on foot, but lost them in the maze of Dumpsters and dead ends in the alleys behind Main Street.

"They got away clean," the deputy said unnecessarily upon his return alone. "Sorry, ma'am."

"Well, your timing was great, anyway," Dallas said, trying to keep both her voice and her knees from trembling. She sat in the back of the cruiser and filled out a police report, but she knew it was useless. She had no descriptions, no identifications, nothing.

There was one thing she saw, or thought she saw, but she didn't include it in the report. She couldn't be sure and, as an officer of the court, she knew she couldn't make an accusation based on something she *thought* she saw.

But when the cruiser had turned its headlights on them, in the instant before she was blinded by the light, Dallas thought she recognized the face of one of the men.

It looked like Petit Cobb.

THE WHITE DOVE of the Desert, usually pale and otherworldly and silent at night, glittered on this night, five days before Christmas, with the sharp lights of dozens of electric candles. From one of the rooms of the old convent school came the shrill, excited voices of children.

Because Dallas was so late picking up Miguel, they arrived after Father Kino's *Las Posadas* celebration had already started. Father Kino met them at the door with two paper cups of pink punch.

"Merry Christmas," he exclaimed, handing one to each of them. "Glad you could make it. Help yourselves to some refreshments—Mrs. Q.'s been cooking all day."

Everywhere Dallas looked she saw children, many of whom she didn't recognize.

Two small, separate Josephs raced around opposite ends of the room, both with their brown robes tucked up into their jeans so as not to trip up their little legs. Two tiny Madonnas, both dressed in blue robes with crowns of artificial flowers secured around their heads, sat in one corner, solemnly swaddling their Baby Jesus dolls.

The Christmas tree was strung with red chili peppers and decorated with the traditional straw figurines made by the Indians. Seeing Reverend Coppersmith standing beside the tree, Dallas suddenly realized that he and Father Kino had somehow managed to bring together the children of the south side and the north side into one, single *posadas* celebration.

Dallas had never heard of such a thing ever having been attempted in Los Reales before.

How wise, she thought wryly. At least the kids wouldn't be carrying knives and guns! She admired the two clergymen for their courage, but she had her doubts about any long-range results. Every generation of children born in Los Reales for the last one hundred years, all as innocent as these, had eventually grown up to be adults just like their parents.

Around the edges of the room sat a few of those parents, obviously the chaperones and drivers for the children Reverend Coppersmith had brought out to the Mission. Most of them seemed ill-at-ease, and many looked at Miguel as though he were some sort of devil in their midst.

Dallas wondered whether they had come of their own accord, or if Reverend Coppersmith had badgered them into it. No matter—they were here, and that in itself was a miracle.

When it came time to break the piñata, Father Kino enlisted Miguel and Dallas's help. She tied the blindfold over the kids' eyes, twirled them around and handed them the long stick. Each, in turn, swung at the piñata that hung from a rope thrown over a low ceiling beam. Miguel worked the rope, lowering the piñata for the little kids, raising it for the taller ones.

He was obviously enjoying himself.

Tonight was the first time she had heard him laugh, and she liked the lighthearted sound. It lifted her own spirits, too, and allowed her to forget, for a little while, the frightful scene in the parking lot.

Finally one of the bigger boys managed to connect with the piñata, and the loud crack sent all the children scurrying to catch the booty that showered to the floor. Miguel hunkered down in their midst, making sure all the kids got a share.

Dallas joined Father Kino and Reverend Coppersmith by the Christmas tree. "How did you manage to pull this off?" she asked.

Both men seemed a little uncertain about the details.

"The thought just came to me tonight while I was at vespers," Father Kino said. "I don't know how or why. God knows I never thought of it before in all these years. But tonight...I don't know, there has been so much unrest in town lately, I..."

He paused, looking suddenly thoughtful. "I had offered my prayers for peace and true Christmas spirit in Los Reales. And then I thought, *of course,* and I called Fred."

"And I'd had the very same idea, as a matter of fact," Reverend Coppersmith continued. "I had been praying myself, when John called. Most of my congregation was unwilling, but as you can see, I managed to coerce a few into coming."

"IT MAY MEAN SOMETHING," Miguel said when Dallas relayed the conversation to him on the drive back to the Quitos' house. "But it can have nothing to do with me. Since I have been here, it seems that things have only become more violent."

"That's not exactly true, Miguel," Dallas protested without much conviction. She had to admit that he might have a point. Certainly, she had never before been confronted the way she had been earlier that evening.

There had always been a few who thought she was abusing her judicial authority by not using it to squelch de Pimas, and their like, at every opportunity. Most northsiders, however, had written her off as a maverick, and were just biding their time until the next election, when Devers would no doubt oppose her, and get their vote.

Now, it seemed, that had changed.

Pa had been more right than she cared to admit. Why had she been so naive as to believe her business was really her own? She had never been hassled before simply because she had never sympathized with the McAllister faction, neither had she done anything to offend them.

Now she had. And in less than a week she had become as much of a pariah on her own side of town as Miguel was.

She glanced over at him, seated beside her in the truck. His face looked, for the moment, content and happy. His face was all she could see of him, due to the children curled up in his lap.

Since they were driving back into town, anyway, Father Kino had asked them to give the Quito grandchildren a ride home. Four-year-old Dolly sat on one of Miguel's knees, and her brother, six-year-old Emilio, on the other. They cuddled against him like a couple of puppies exhausted from play.

When she pulled up in front of the Quito farmhouse, Miguel carried the tiny girl into the house and Dallas followed, supporting the boy on his stumbling feet. Once into the bedroom the children shared, where they removed their jackets and grungy little sneakers, they eased the children into their bunk beds, and covered them with quilts.

Quietly they closed the bedroom door and tiptoed out.

"Do you have to leave right away?" Miguel asked.

"No, not at all," Dallas replied, glad for an excuse not to have to do exactly that.

"Here, come sit on the couch." Taking her hand, he led her into the darkened living room and seated her on the sofa. "I have something I want to show you," he said mysteriously.

With that, he sat down on the sofa beside her, picked up the remote control for the television set, and switched it on. Immediately the screen flickered to life with a very antiquated sitcom.

"What do you think of that?" he demanded, smiling broadly as he fixed his gaze on the screen.

"Of... what?" she began blankly. "Oh, you mean the *television set?*"

"Yes! A miracle, isn't it? Dolly and Emilio said the pictures come from the sky." Leaning back into the cushions, he draped a companionable arm across Dallas's shoulders, then started flipping through the channels. "Have you ever seen anything like this?"

"Well, yes, as a matter of fact. I have one at home in my bedroom. Most people have a TV."

Miguel looked amazed. "Dolly and Emilio didn't tell me that. You mean most people have these miracle boxes in their homes and they don't even *talk* about them? They just take them for granted?''

"Mostly they use them to *avoid* talking," Dallas replied with a grin. ''But, yes, we do tend to take television pretty much for granted, I guess.''

"A miracle. Your world is full of miracles, Dallas. Do you know that? A lifetime would not be enough to understand all the new things there are.''

They *were* miracles, she guessed, in a way—televisions, telephones, electricity, automobiles. Where once the cattlemen and the Indians had killed each other over water rights, even the simple fact that there was now water enough in the desert for all who lived here was a miracle.

Dallas admired the way Miguel met this new world in which he found himself—not warily, not suspiciously, but with eagerness and wonder. She wondered if she would have been able to cope so well, if she'd somehow been turned back in time to his world. She doubted it.

Sighing a little, she moved closer into the curve of his arm. It felt good, it felt *right* to be next to him like this, to feel the warmth of his solid forearm behind her neck, the steady rise and fall of his chest beside her.

In the few short days she'd known him, he had become so much a part of her life that she could hardly remember a time when he wasn't there. He was her first thought in the morning, and her last before falling off to sleep at night.

In a strange way, she felt as though he had always been with her, a part of herself that she had only just realized existed, but that had been there all along.

She tried not to think about how quickly the days were passing. In five days it would be Christmas Eve. And if Christmas was the deadline for whatever Miguel was supposed to accomplish—if indeed he was supposed to accomplish anything at all, and his presence in this time wasn't just an accident of Fate—time was running out.

If it had something to do with Father Sebastiani's angry proclamation, which was the only theory they had come up with, his presence in Los Reales certainly hadn't poured oil over any troubled waters yet.

Miguel heard the sigh. "You are thinking that I will not have a lifetime to spend in this world."

Dallas sighed again. "I just wish we knew, that's all. If we knew, at least we could make some plans...."

He rested his chin on top of her head. She felt his warm breath tickling her skin through her crisp red curls.

"What plans would you make, *querida mia,* if we knew what is in the future for us?"

Dallas considered the question carefully. "Well, we could leave, just go, and leave all this insanity behind. We could start fresh somewhere else, where it wouldn't matter that you're de Pima and I'm McAllister. Where no one would care..."

"You would leave your home for me?"

"Yes. I'd love to leave Los Reales. Sometimes I think I hate it here."

"If that is true, why have you not left already?"

Dallas had considered that question before. She had no answer for it. "I did leave once. But I . . . had to come back. I'm not sure why."

There was the land, of course—the extensive McAllister holdings that had belonged to the family for more than one hundred years, and which someday would be hers.

But that wasn't the only reason. She loved the vastness of the Sonoran Desert—the ragged peaks of its mountains, the subtlety of its forms and colors found nowhere else on earth, the cold, clear air of its winters, and the challenge of its scorching summers.

But there was something else, too. It was something deep within her that she could neither put into words nor understand.

She felt as though she was waiting for something.

Sometimes she got restless, like a migratory bird as the change of season grows nearer, but just as its instincts won't let it act until the time is right, neither could hers.

"My roots are here, I guess," she finished simply, trying to distill her nebulous thoughts into one succinct sentence.

Dallas felt the muscle of his forearm tighten behind her neck. "But you would leave for me?"

"I think I'd be happy living anywhere with you."

"*Querida mia*, you would marry me?"

Dallas raised her face toward him. "If I were to live with you, I would definitely insist on being married to you," she said with a teasing smile.

After avoiding this commitment for all of her life, she made it now as if it were as natural as breathing. How clear, she thought incredulously. How uncomplicated, when it was right!

Miguel felt his body come to life. For the first time since his return, he felt himself fully a man. Looking down into her sparkling blue eyes, his own dark ones smoldered.

"My little white dove," he said thickly, reaching back one hundred years in his memory for the name he had once given Dorthea. With one hand, he cupped Dallas's upturned face, and held it while he covered her mouth with his.

Her lips were so soft, so sweet, so *familiar* beneath his. And her body, as she instinctively pressed it against him, was warm and willing, and also achingly familiar. He inhaled the scent of her hair, and his fingers entangled themselves in its full, flowing masses.

Tightening his hands, he caught two fistsful of hair on either side of her face, holding her prisoner by means of her own hair while his moist lips tasted her cheeks, her eyelids, her neck.

In the name of God, Miguel thought in an agony of savage pleasure, even if he could not stay, it was worth it, it was worth everything, just to hold this fiery-haired, fiery-natured woman one more time.

To feel this way. One more time.

Dallas slid lower on the sofa, and her arms, wrapped around Miguel's shoulders, urged him down on top of her.

Not here, not now. Dallas knew that. Not with children sleeping down the hall, and their grandparents just a little farther than that. Still, she yearned desperately to prolong this feeling she had never known before, this passion that was overtaking her like a drug.

With a groan, Miguel seized her wrists in his two hands and resolutely removed them from his shoulders. "We must stop, before it is too late," he muttered fiercely.

"It's already too late." *Our time's come 'round again,* suggested the voice with the slightest Scot's brogue that seemed, in the past few days, to have taken up residence in Dallas's head. She thought of it as Dorthea's voice. *Dinna make me live without ye again.* "Come home with me tonight."

"*Querida,* I cannot!" Miguel looked uncomfortable at the suggestion, but also full of regret. "It is a sin that we should love each other that way outside of marriage." He sounded as though he was reciting a catechism he had memorized word for word, but was no longer sure of its meaning. "I will not dishonor you that way."

Dinna speak t'me aboot honor, Dorthea's voice scoffed. *What dishonor is there in love?*

"And what if there should be a child?" Miguel continued. "You would be disgraced forever, and so would the child."

But at least then I'd ha' somethin' left of ye, Dorthea argued. And very persuasively, Dallas thought.

But once the fever had cooled a bit, she was as bewildered by her own actions as she had been that night in Gila Bend. She wondered if Miguel would believe that she had never thrown herself at any other man before in her life. She could hardly believe it herself.

Smoothing her tangled hair into some semblance of order, Dallas shakily got to her feet. "I guess I'd better go before I make an even bigger fool of myself," she said, and forced an upbeat smile to her lips.

Miguel was by her side in an instant. "You are not a fool," he contradicted in a harsh whisper. In a gesture that contradicted everything he'd said about honor and God's law, he took her face in his hands and kissed her fiercely.

"Don't ever think that!" he commanded. "If I am allowed to stay in your world, believe me, you will never spend another night alone in your bed for the rest of our lives."

"And if you're not?" Dallas whispered above the sound of her pounding heart.

Slowly, reluctantly, Miguel let his hands fall from her face. His shoulders twisted in a fatalistic shrug. "If I am not allowed to stay, then I have no future. There is no need to make plans about that."

Together they walked out the Quitos' front door. The porch light was burned out, and Miguel held Dallas firmly around her waist, as if she might not be able to find her way across the porch and down the few rickety steps without his help.

The proximity of their bodies, the brushing of their thighs against each other as they walked, created an intimacy almost as intense as that which had begun then ended too quickly in the Quitos' living room.

The Quitos didn't waste pricey water on non-essentials, so the tiny yard in front of their farmhouse was made up of gravel and sand, and a few sickly clumps of patchy scrub grass. It was terrain as treacherous as the rickety porch steps, or so Miguel seemed to think, because his arm remained tightly around Dallas's waist until they reached the unpaved road where her truck was parked.

Where, under the moon and the starlight of the clear desert night, they saw that all four of her tires had been slashed.

Chapter Eleven

"And they work on their motorcycles in the front yard, and they killed all the grass. And the whole place is full of grease and rags and auto parts. They sit in the garage all night and drink beer, and play their music so loud no one can get any sleep. Then the neighbors call me and *I* can't get any sleep!"

Dallas shuffled through the stack of papers on her desk and came up with an affidavit filed by one Matthew Macaffee. She read through it.

"Your tenant's lease has expired, you say, Mr. Macaffee?" she asked.

"Four months ago, Your Honor!" Mr. Macaffee sputtered. "But they won't go! And they ain't paying the rent anymore, neither—not that they was much better before. This is a decent, family neighborhood, Your Honor. Working folks. Nice yards. Kids. I want this trash off my property!"

Dallas reached into a drawer and pulled out a form, which she signed and handed to the man standing before her desk.

Mr. Macaffee looked at it uncomprehendingly. "A Notice of Eviction?" he read aloud. "But . . . an *eviction notice?* What good's this gonna do me?"

"It's legal notification that your tenants are required to vacate the property, Mr. Macaffee."

"Yeah, but so what? Who's gonna make 'em go? I need some muscle . . . like maybe a few deputies."

"That's a court order, Mr. Macaffee. It means your tenants have to vacate your premises. If they don't, they'll be in contempt of court, and we can use more stringent methods—"

"Beggin' your pardon, Your Honor," the man said, flapping the piece of paper nervously between his fingers. "But they ain't gonna pay no mind to this, especially . . ."

"Especially—what?" Dallas repeated, mystified.

"Well, especially when it's comin' from you," the man said reluctantly.

Then his voice rose defiantly. "Sorry, Your Honor, but that's the way it is, and you might's well know it. With what's been goin' on . . . with the Indian and all, I mean . . ."

"Exactly what *do* you mean, Mr. Macaffee?"

Mr. Macaffee shuffled his feet in embarrassment. "Well, there's some in town talkin' about impeachment, that's all. I don't think this here eviction notice's gonna do anything but get me beat up."

Impeachment? Dallas looked up at Mr. Macaffee, frowning. Behind him she could see her nearly deserted courtroom. Dust motes floated in the weak sunlight that filtered in through the window.

So *that* was the reason most of the defendants on her docket hadn't shown up for their appearances, she thought sourly, surveying the room with a jaundiced eye.

In the first row sat old Mabel Abbott with an injured cat in her lap and an injured look on her face. Behind her, Cora McAllister clutched her purse with one hand, and with the other, the arm of her son, Georgie, caught shoplifting at the five-and-dime.

They were newcomers to her courtroom and obviously still in awe of the judicial system, whereas the regulars had apparently adopted a more cynical attitude. If indeed an impeachment petition was being circulated, and certainly Mr. Macaffee had no reason to lie, they were probably gambling that the next J.P. might be less . . . *familiar* . . . with their assorted predilections.

"An eviction notice is the first step in the process, Mr. Macaffee," Dallas said coldly to the antsy landlord standing before her. "I'm afraid you're going to have to give it a try. If you run into a problem, give my office a call."

She dismissed him more curtly than she'd intended.

Don't kill the messenger, she reminded herself.

It isn't Matthew Macaffee's fault that the whole town has gone crazy. Impeachment?

After last night, she really should have expected something like this.

The sheriff's department had taken considerable time to respond to her call—not long enough to make Dallas think they were dilly-dallying on purpose, but just long enough to make her wonder.

When the two gum-cracking deputies had finally shown up and found her standing with Miguel beside the vandalized truck, they'd seemed barely able to conceal their glee over the compromising situation.

They had been deferential to a fault, so much so that it had been obviously a travesty, and they'd kept calling her *Ms.* McAllister and Miguel *Mr.* de Pima.

You say you live *here, Mr. de Pima? Do you have any* proof *of that?*

But what were you doing *out here on the south side so* late *at night, Ms. McAllister?*

Their voices had been solicitous enough, Dallas supposed, and the questions routine, but between questions and answers, she'd seen the two catch each other's eye and smirk. Both long-term veterans of the Los Reales Sheriff's Department, they'd acted like two little boys sharing a smutty joke.

And by the morning, Dallas knew without a doubt, they would have shared the joke with every other little boy in the station house. By the morning, the entire locker room would be teeming with sniggering speculation about her availability and her sexual preferences. The very thought put her teeth on edge.

She'd felt compromised. She'd felt soiled. And she'd hated herself for having allowed the two louts to make her feel that way.

Maybe she shouldn't have called them, she realized now, but in her world—the McAllister world—it was second nature to call the police when there was trouble. As long as she had lived in Los Reales, as long as she had been justice of the peace, she had never quite understood that things were very different on the south side of town.

It was frightening. And infuriating. She resolved to rectify the untenable situation as soon as possible— but at the time she had had to get out of the immediate untenable situation in which she'd found herself.

Having wrapped up their report, a report that Dallas knew would never be followed up, the deputies had hot-footed it back to their cruiser.

Haughtily, Dallas had lifted her chin. She'd turned to Miguel. "I'm going to get a lift home with these deputies. I'm sure they won't mind."

She'd glanced over her shoulder. "Will you, fellas?" she'd said in a voice that broached no discussion; after all, she was still the J.P.

Turning back to Miguel, she'd added, "I'll send a tow for the truck tomorrow morning."

"You will be all right?" he'd asked in a low voice.

"I'll be all right," Dallas had assured him. Then, impulsively, she'd risen up on tiptoe and kissed him on the cheek. "Thanks for a lovely evening," she'd said softly.

The deputies nearly had choked on their chewing gum.

Might as well be hung for a sheep as a lamb, she'd thought defiantly as she'd climbed into the seat behind the officers and felt the cruiser speed away....

Mr. Macaffee exited the courtroom, muttering under his breath. "Next case," Dallas called abruptly, pounding her gavel on the desk.

Old Mabel Abbott got stiffly to her feet, cradling her bandaged cat like a baby, and approached the desk to lodge her grievance.

A MAN COULD get used to this, Miguel said to himself as he steered Dallas's truck confidently down Main Street. He headed directly for her office next door to city hall, and when he arrived there, pointed the truck at the curbside parking meter and squealed to a halt.

Dallas heard the squeal and looked up to see a chrome grill advancing at breakneck speed toward her window. That was the first shock—the second was realizing that it was the chrome grill of *her* truck.

"My God, Miguel," she cried, tearing out the door. "What are you *doing?*"

"Driving," he replied proudly. "The tow truck never came, and I think the Quitos did not want the truck sitting out in front of their house. So Beginio went into town and bought new tires and put them on. He showed me how to make it go and how to make it stop—the rest I figured out for myself."

One hand on her chest, Dallas tried to slow her racing heart. "Please don't do it again," she said breathlessly. "At least not until I can give you a few lessons. I thought you were going to come right through my window!"

"But I didn't," Miguel pointed out with incontrovertible logic.

"No, you didn't," Dallas had to admit, laughing. "But it's still against the law to drive a motor vehicle without a license. I fine people enormous amounts of money every day for doing exactly that."

Miguel's eyebrows arched skeptically. "I would think that would be the least of the crimes you have to worry about in Los Reales."

He was wearing new clothes. Plain but shiny new boots, and Levi's that hugged his sinewy legs, brought his appearance right up into the twentieth century.

Very up-to-date, Dallas thought approvingly. She felt a visceral quiver in the pit of her stomach that had nothing to do with the new clothes, but everything to do with what was beneath them.

"I like your new clothes," she told him.

Miguel looked pleased. "Father Kino has given me pay for working at the Mission. He suggested I buy some new boots with it. He said I could not work in the ones I had—if I cut off a toe or something, he said the Mission's insurance wouldn't cover me."

Miguel looked confused. "I don't know what he meant by that, but he laughed like it was a joke."

Dallas laughed, too. "It *was* a joke, Miguel. But the boots were a good idea."

"But so much money! The whole Papago tribe could live for a year on the money these boots cost!"

"Not everything's changed for the better," Dallas said. And *that* was not a joke. Even in Los Reales, the stresses of modern life were felt.

The state and county governments seemed to just be waiting for the town to dry up and blow away, maybe become another ghost town that could be turned into a tourist attraction. After all, it was the oldest American settlement in the Tucson Valley. But for some reason no one could explain, the oldest American settlement in the Tucson Valley kept on keeping on.

"...and Mrs. Quito gave me some clothes," Miguel was continuing. "They belonged to her son, Horatio, the father of the two little ones who live with her. She says she hasn't heard from Horatio for a long time, and to consider the clothes an early Christmas gift."

"They fit you very well," Dallas said. She wondered if Horatio had looked as good in his clothes as Miguel did. "And you cut your hair."

The bandanna was no longer tied around his head; instead his hair hung straight and blunt to just above his collar, emphasizing the square lines of his features.

"That was Mrs. Quito's idea, too. She said it was time I stopped looking like a...a...*hippie*." He paused, looking puzzled. "What is a *hippie?*"

Dallas smiled. "Come on inside and I'll explain it to you."

"Wait." Miguel stayed her with a hand on her arm. "I think we should talk out here."

She looked at him questioningly.

"Last night, when you kissed me—in front of those two deputies, I thought that maybe you were trying to tell me something."

"Trying to tell you—what?"

Miguel shrugged. "I am not sure. Maybe that you were done playing by the rules of Los Reales. Maybe that you were done with...secrets."

Last night she had felt humiliated. Last night she had been outraged. Last night, for possibly the first time in her life, she had experienced the constraints of the feud up front and personal.

Had she also made the commitment last night to fight it?

A determined expression narrowed her eyes. She flashed Miguel a resolute smile that sealed a pact she hadn't even realized she was proposing. Miguel was right, she thought. It was time—long past time—to stop pussyfooting around.

"I guess I was," she said. "Where do we start?"

They started with a slow stroll down Main Street, looking in the windows of the shops that were closed for lunch, admiring the Christmas decorations that hung from the streetlights and holding hands.

They stopped in Chauncy's Twenty-Four-Hour Diner for take-out hamburgers, fries and coffee, then walked to the town square, where they ate and drank on a park bench beneath the twenty-foot tumbleweed Christmas tree that adorned the plaza.

People gaped at them but said nothing, except for a little girl who had been one of the tiny Madonnas at Father Kino's *posadas* celebration.

"Hi, Dallas. Hi, Miguel," she said shyly, before her mother jerked her away.

Even the young bucks at Chauncy's—Devers, Wyatt, Petit—had been speechless. They had only watched, dumbfounded, as Dallas had introduced Miguel to an openmouthed Chauncy and ordered food to go.

After finishing lunch, Dallas and Miguel went back to Dallas's office on the opposite side of the street, so that she could stop in with the sheriff, ostensibly to inquire whether there was any new information regarding her vandalized truck.

"Whew, I feel like I've run a gauntlet!" she exclaimed once they had returned to the dusty truck.

"Are you sorry?"

Dallas grinned. "Not for a minute," she said vehemently. "In fact—" unlocking her office door, she reached inside to close the blinds and switch off the lights "—since we're on a roll, I think we should go shake up the south side a little bit, too."

DALLAS CRUISED slowly down First Street, which had indeed been the first and, during its earlier years, the only street in Los Reales.

It was the street of gunfights and shoot-outs, of U.S. marshals using violence to combat violence, of saloons and gambling casinos and brothels.

The "Wild West" was long gone now. First Street was paved, of course. The brothels were gone and gunfights were rare. The saloons and gambling casinos were gone, too, although Dallas knew that illegal slot machines and card games still flourished, just as they did on Main Street in the back room of Big Lil's.

First Street and Main Street were, in fact, virtually indistinguishable from one another, as were the people who trod them, hurrying from shop to shop, intent on completing their Christmas shopping.

But First Street had one thing Main didn't. At its center, in place of the town square, it had the presidio, an old Spanish fort whose thick walls had provided protection from marauding Apaches to the early settlers of the Tucson Valley.

The presidio was a ruin now, its original reason for existence having been swept away by the tides of history. Now it was part of the plaza for those who lived on the south side.

Its ruined walls and open courtyards, most of which had once been covered by ceilings, were lush with bougainvillea blossoms and dark green cat's claw. An ancient mesquite sent its gnarled branches over, around and through the thick adobe walls.

And everywhere woody-stemmed poinsettias, their roots as ancient as the old mesquite, waved their flamboyant red leaves in celebration of the Christmas season.

The presidio had a gracious, Old World charm, Dallas thought, much more interesting than the banal respectability of Los Reales's official town square on the other side of town.

Dallas parked the truck on a side street, then she and Miguel walked into the presidio.

Cat's claw vines climbed over the entrance to the fort, where massive wooden gates had once swung wide to admit horses, soldiers and supply wagons. On the lintel hung a twinkling tinsel Christmas star.

The open stockyard, where visiting dignitaries, presidents and Indian delegations had been received, where floggings had been administered, and executions carried out, was now a small, green park equipped with an automatic sprinkler system to keep the patchy grass alive.

Wild green parrots from the Chiricahua Mountains screamed in the trees. There were children everywhere, climbing the old walls and swinging on tires hanging from the branches of the rambling mesquite.

As they strolled along the broken tile floors of the inner courtyards, Miguel, feeling more relaxed on this side of town, draped a companionable arm over Dallas's shoulder.

Dallas, on the other hand, felt less relaxed. People stared at her with blank, brown eyes. Some seemed curious, but most were just suspicious. She felt vulnerable, like some ignorant outsider who had inadvertently invaded their territory and didn't even have the sense to realize nobody wanted her here.

It was not a feeling she had experienced before in her life and it made her uncomfortable.

This is where bigotry comes from, she thought. One group of people feels uncomfortable with another's unfamiliar people and customs, and wrongly blames the other group for those uncomfortable feelings. After a while, you have a situation like the one in Los Reales.

But somehow being with Miguel that afternoon almost made her forget Los Reales's troubles and restored some genuine Christmas hope. When the late afternoon turned cool, Dallas was a little sad when Miguel suggested they might want to go back to the truck.

AFTER A LESS than auspicious beginning, the day had turned out better than Dallas could ever have anticipated.

"Want to get something to eat before we head back to the Quitos'?" she proposed hopefully, hating to see it end.

"There is something else I have to tell you first," Miguel said. His voice was somber. "I will not be going back to the Quitos'. I have decided to return to the Mission."

"But why? The Quitos seem very happy to have you there."

"A rock was thrown through their front window last night. There was a note tied around it. It said 'Traitor.'"

The sun still shone. The sky was still cloudless and blue overhead. The dry desert wind still sifted through the sand along the edges of the sidewalk and the street. But somehow the day had turned suddenly sinister.

"Oh, Miguel, I'm so sorry. Was anyone hurt?"

"No. But I do not wish to endanger them further. This is not a fight they have chosen. And then, there are the children...."

Dallas shivered. "Of course. The children..."

In the rearview mirror, she watched the presidio retreat into the background.

The ice-cream man still pushed his white cart with its red-and-white striped umbrella. Children in bright clothing still danced around him.

The late afternoon sun slanted at a sharp angle, a paintbrush tinting the mesquite and the cactus and the brilliant red poinsettias with shades of gold.

Dallas felt rather as though she were looking at the scene through a camera lens gone out of focus. It looked the same, only it was somehow different. All the radiant fiesta colors were smudged with the drab shade of violence.

"Of course, the children," she repeated. She turned to Miguel. "Don't go to the Mission," she said suddenly. "Come stay with me."

He shook his head. "No, I cannot—I *will not* put you in that danger."

"Miguel, don't you see? I'm already in danger, and so are you! A rock could come through my window, too, you know."

"It would be much more likely to happen if I am there than if I am at the Mission," Miguel said emphatically.

"But still, it could happen. And it would be so much less *frightening* if you were there with me—if I knew at least that you were safe. The Mission is so isolated. If there were a problem out there, who would know?"

She placed her hand on Miguel's arm and gave him a sweet, persuasive smile. "Please?"

Miguel looked at her helplessly. It had been a long time—one hundred years, in one way—since he had been confronted with the irresistible McAllister willfulness. He found that his susceptibility hadn't lessened with time.

It had been difficult enough to keep himself from going to her that night in the motel at Gila Bend, especially when he'd been achingly aware of how much she'd wanted him, too. Would he be able to impose that kind of discipline on himself night after night?

He wanted to refuse.

He wanted to tell her that she would be better off without him, better off if she would permit him to go to the Mission and disappear from her life; but he suddenly realized that, although it might be the right thing to do, disappearing from her life was the last thing in the world he wanted to do.

Besides, it was possible that she truly would be in danger. He could not bear to think of not being with her if something should happen and she needed him.

"Very well, *querida mia*," he sighed, throwing up his hands in defeat. "I will stay with you."

God takes care of fools and children, Father Sebastiani used to say. Miguel fervently hoped it was true.

Chapter Twelve

Dinner, Dallas remembered belatedly as they walked in her front door.

"Make yourself comfortable," she told Miguel as she disappeared into the tiny kitchenette. "I'll just be a minute."

And a minute was just about all the time it took for her to decide that neither the frozen dinners nor the single package of hot dogs, nor the yogurts and diet colas populating the shelves of her refrigerator, would make a dent in any man's appetite.

Then she inspected the cupboard. No surprises there, either.

She leaned against the breakfast bar, drumming her fingers impatiently on the white Formica, while she tried to figure out how she could create the gourmet meal she would like to prepare for Miguel out of a few cans of chili and a package of frozen hot dogs.

MIGUEL SAT DOWN on a tan *equipales* couch—the traditional leather-and-woven-willow furniture, made in Mexico, that had been common throughout the Southwest even in the old days. The soft leather molded itself around him as if it already knew the shape of his body.

He liked Dallas's home.

Windows on three sides opened onto the desert and brought it inside. Skylights in the vaulted ceilings brought the sky inside, too. The tiled floors and white walls gave it a clean, open feeling, adding to the sense that the inside and the outside were one and the same.

He liked the colorful Indian blankets scattered on the tile and hung here and there on the walls. They were woven by the Navaho tribe from the north, and traded, in his time at least, for the salt his people gathered at the Gulf of Mexico.

The Indian blankets, the tiles, the *equipales* furniture he recognized. But there were other things that he couldn't begin to understand. For example, there was no fireplace, nor a wood stove, and Miguel didn't catch the slightest hint of wood smoke. Yet the house was warm.

"Dallas," he called in her direction, "how is it that you can have heat with no fire?"

Dallas poked her head out of the kitchen. "Not only do we have heat without fire today, but we also have air-conditioning in the summer, so it stays nice and cool indoors, even when the desert is one-hundred-twenty degrees."

Then, of course, she had to show him the miracle of the thermostat, and tell as much as she knew about its operation. She only wished she had a more mechanical brain so that she could explain in greater detail, for his curiosity was insatiable.

To make amends for her lack of technical information, she turned on the television, which she knew intrigued Miguel.

She didn't know much about its operation, either. The explanation the Quitos' grandchildren had given him—that the pictures came from the sky—suited her just fine; but Miguel so enjoyed channel-surfing with the remote control that he wasn't, for the moment, interested in more specific information.

"I have another miracle to show you," she teased.

Picking up the telephone, she touch-toned a number as indelibly imprinted in her memory as 9-1-1.

In exactly nineteen minutes, while Dallas assembled tableware and drinks, the delivery boy from the Twenty-Minutes-Or-It's-On-Us Pizza Parlor on Main Street was at the door. He always made it in exactly nineteen minutes—no more, no less. Dallas often wondered if he waited in his car until the last possible moment, just to get the customers' hopes up.

She sat down beside Miguel and put the hot cardboard box on the coffee table. "Food delivered hot right to your door. How's *that* for a miracle?"

When she opened the lid, the air was filled with a variety of aromas Miguel had never encountered in combination before.

"It's got everything on it," Dallas told him. "Tomatoes, cheese, pepperoni, sausage, onions, olives, anchovies—you name it, it's in there."

"Garlic?"

"Absolutely," she confirmed what his nose had already told him. "What do you think?"

Miguel nibbled experimentally at the edges. "Hot," he ventured. He took a larger bite.

"I like it!" he exclaimed, then made quick work of the rest of the slice, singeing his mouth in the process. He took another piece and devoured it as quickly. "What is it?"

"It's called pizza. It's Italian."

"Italian?"

"From Italy. That's a country in Europe—"

"Ah, I remember. Yes, Father Sebastiani spoke of it. Not far from his own homeland, he'd said. But he never spoke of this pizza!"

"Actually, I don't think it had been invented yet. But even if they did have it, it couldn't have been this good. I don't think they knew how to make gluey cheese and dehydrated onions and freeze-dried sausage in those days."

Miguel stopped chewing long enough to look at her quizzically from over his pizza slice.

Dallas laughed. "Just a joke," she said.

She enjoyed introducing him to new things. He was so curious about the changes one hundred years had wrought, as if he wanted to learn as much as possible in whatever length of time he had to spend here.

He took such pleasure in the small day-to-day things that everyone else took for granted. And when she was with him, she looked at them the same way. The world was indeed filled with miracles. Why hadn't she seen them until he'd come into her life?

After clearing away the remnants of pizza and coffee, Dallas closed all the drapes, which shut out the streetlights and created an instant coziness in the room. Then she returned to the couch and sat down beside Miguel. He turned on the television, put his arm around her and pulled her closer, but not as close as he had last night at the Quitos'.

Disappointment washed over her. She had hoped for an encore performance.

Miguel had finally landed on Channel Three, where an Animated Film Festival was in progress.

Although she tried to fix her attention on the images that seemed to have entranced Miguel, she found that her eyes kept returning to things closer at hand.

Like the warmth of the thigh that pressed into her own from knee to hip.

Like the long expanse of legs she could see from the corner of her eye, the ankle of one propped on the knee of the other, with an intriguing vee of tan leather at their juncture.

Like the taut muscles that flexed every time he changed position the slightest bit.

And he shifted position often, as if he couldn't quite get comfortable. He crossed and recrossed his legs. He fidgeted a little to the left and then back to the right.

He lowered his arm from the back of the couch to rest momentarily on her shoulder, then moved it up again.

He was nervous, she realized; as nervous as she was. She wondered if it was due to the same reason.

Did he feel the intimate warmth where their thighs touched, denim-to-denim?

Did he want to drop his arm again to her shoulder, and from there to her arms, where it might graze her breast?

That's what she wanted. That, and much, much more.

But raised in a different time, with different customs, what was it that Miguel wanted?

Even knowing how much she wanted him, would he make love to her, especially believing as he did that making love outside of marriage would dishonor a woman. It was definitely a minority opinion these days, but not altogether displeasing, whether you called it doing right or just called it discriminating.

But for the first time in her life, Dallas was ready more than ready—eager!—to invite a man into her bed. And she found that she didn't know how to make it happen. She knew little about making the first move.

All she knew for sure was that she had been ready to make love with him since she had first set eyes on him. Possibly, in some strange, inexplicable way, even before that.

Ragged and dirty and confused though he'd been, something in her had recognized him.

And she also was sure that if she lost him, she'd spend the rest of her life waiting for him to come back.

Miguel shifted again on the couch. He took his left foot down from his right knee, then immediately propped his right foot on his left knee. In the process, he pulled Dallas a little closer into the crook of his arm, so close that she was sure she could hear his heart beating. Or maybe it was her own, chasing her blood through every vein and artery and capillary in her body until she could feel it pounding in her temples.

Glancing up at Miguel, she saw that his eyes were fixed on the television screen. She wanted to touch him, hold him, pull him down on top of her so that she could feel his chest hard against hers, against the softness of her breasts that suddenly ached for his touch, the way she had that night at the Quitos'.

Instead, with a ragged sigh, she returned her attention to the animated film. She found that she had no idea in the world why the stuttering rabbit was hammering the lisping duck into the ground like a nail.

When the film ended, Dallas regretfully reminded herself that tomorrow was a workday.

"It's getting late," she said in a reluctant voice.

Miguel looked at her, startled, then at the television screen.

For an instant he seemed surprised to see that the film was over, then he took a deep breath and forced himself to visibly relax. Dallas had the fleeting but distinct impression that if she quizzed him about the stuttering rabbit and the squawking duck with a speech impediment, he'd have no more idea what they'd been up to than she did.

Well, hadn't she told him that people used television to avoid *talking?* she mused with a twist of her lips. And other things, she added.

"I guess we'd better start thinking about going to bed," she continued in the same reluctant tone.

"I will sleep on your couch, then?" Miguel asked.

Dallas flushed. "If that's what you want."

Miguel looked at her across the few inches that separated them. He smiled ruefully. "It is *not* what I want. What I want I know I have no right to want."

He took Dallas's chin between his thumb and forefinger and tilted her head upward, then he pressed his mouth to hers.

It was a gentle kiss, but Dallas felt heat behind it, felt passion straining to break through. She parted her lips, but he only skirted her mouth with his tongue, tasting, not allowing himself to completely indulge his hunger.

"I said I would not leave another beautiful woman crying," he told her solemnly. "But I think it is too late for that now."

Dallas's breath caught. Any reference to time these past few days always reminded her of how quickly was passing. "Too late?" she repeated in a panicked voice. "Too late for what? Have you remembered something?"

"No, *querida mia*. I mean only that I know in my heart that you love me—"

"I already *said* I would marry you," she replied, laughing shakily. "That should have told you *something.*"

Miguel smiled, then kissed her again. "And you know in your heart that I love you. I believe that I have always loved you. But—" His voice sounded reflexive, almost as if he were talking to himself. "To leave you, as I left Dorthea, knowing the suffering she endured because of me—"

"Miguel, did you ever think that maybe a little, tiny part of the reason Dorthea was so devastated by your death was because she knew she had lost you, when she had never completely *had* you?"

Miguel looked at her sharply.

"She had to go through her whole life never knowing the fulfillment, the ... *completion* of making love with the only man she ever loved. If it were me, that's how I'd feel. Think about it."

Smiling enigmatically, Dallas gently disengaged herself from his encircling arm. She went into her bedroom, returning a few moments later with a blanket and pillow. During that short round trip, another idea presented itself.

"You know, Miguel," she said, standing in front of him with the bedclothes clutched in her arms. "Now that I think about it, I wonder..."

She hesitated, suddenly abashed, feeling as though she were prying into something that was none of her business. But she needed to know. She needed to know everything there was to know about him.

"Have you ever *made* love to a woman before?" she blurted. An embarrassed flush crept up her neck to her face. Every freckle was afloat in a sea of red.

Miguel aimed the remote control at the television and switched it off. Then he gave Dallas a bemused quirk of his straight, thin lips. "Is that the reason you think I do not make love to you?"

"Well, I mean, I'm just curious," she replied, feeling more naive by the minute. "I know you didn't with Dorthea. And I know you aren't the kind of man who'd go to a brothel...." She shrugged her shoulders, aiming for nonchalance, but didn't retract her question.

"You're so interested in learning about the world today," she said in defense of her curiosity. "I'm just as interested in how things—things like that, for example—were handled back then. I mean, men and women today fall into bed at the drop of a hat. They get a lot of practice...."

Miguel smiled. "A lot of practice?" he repeated meditatively, as if he were giving his reply a great deal of thought. "You are asking me if I...*know how* to make love to a woman?"

His smile broadened further.

"Believe me, *querida,* even with no practice, the doing of it comes with no difficulty at all. If, as you say, men and women today make love at the drop of a hat, surely you have learned that. But if you are truly interested in how such things were handled in my time

I can only tell you that different men handled it in different ways. As for me—I was married.''

"Married?" Dallas echoed. She was so surprised that the embarrassed flush quickly receded, leaving her freckles beached once again in her pale skin. "But you've never said a word about that!"

"It was a very long time ago."

As she watched, Miguel pushed himself up from the tan *equipales* couch. He walked to the patio door, where he pulled back a handful of drapes and stared out at the clear desert night.

"No one went unmarried long in those days," he began. "Her name was Paio. She was fifteen and I was seventeen when Father Sebastiani married us."

"Were you in love?"

"We were children. What did we know of love? A man needs a woman and a woman needs a man—no one spoke of love. It was later, with Dorthea, that I learned about love."

"What happened to your wife?"

"She died. In childbirth. She was seventeen."

"I'm so sorry, Miguel."

"But my son lived. He was raised by his mother's family—that was the custom among our people—but I provided for him."

She didn't know what to say. It was a tragedy, albeit one that occurred with sad regularity, in these days as well as in those.

To her, the people he spoke of were no more real than names in a history book, but to Miguel they were flesh and blood, and that made her care about them, too. "You were so young...why didn't you marry again?"

"There was no time. Our way of life was changing. The Americans moved into the territory. They brought cattle, and cattle require much land and much water. So they claimed more and more of the land we had lived on forever, and forced us to leave. There was no work. Many of our people were driven out. My wife's family went to Indian Oasis. I hired on with The McAllister. The next year I met Dorthea."

"And your son?"

"I never saw him after he went to Indian Oasis."

A lump rose in Dallas's throat. Ancient history, she thought again; but to the man standing in front of her, only ten days ago.

To him, these wounds were still raw. He was still mourning the life he had left behind, the people he loved who were dead. Not only dead, but long dead, so long dead that no one but Miguel even remembered that they had walked the earth at all.

How lonely he must be, she thought.

She understood now why he had said he could never forgive. It was unfair of God, or Fate, or whatever power it was in the universe that had done this thing to him, to *require* that he forgive.

Why had Father Sebastiani added that part about forgiveness to the curse he'd put on Los Reales? she wondered.

"Miguel, I don't know what to say. I'm sorry I made you remember, if it makes you sad."

"To remember Paio no longer makes me sad. Only sometimes . . . I wonder about the boy. I wonder if he lived to grow up."

Dallas blinked tears from her eyes. She dropped the blanket and pillow on the sofa, then joined Miguel at the patio door.

Laying her cheek against his back, she slipped her arms around his waist. "I'm so sorry," she said again.

Not knowing what else to say, feeling Miguel lost in the past, she kissed him between his shoulder blades and left him alone with his memories.

Chapter Thirteen

Sometime during the night, Dallas sensed the presence of another person in her bedroom.

Turning over with a sleepy sigh, she saw a man standing at the foot of her bed. She wasn't for a moment frightened. The figure standing there had been so much a part of her dreams for the past week that she wasn't sure whether or not she was still dreaming.

His silhouette was dark, so shadowed that she couldn't make out his face, but she could see that he was wearing only a pair of jeans. She realized she was awake, for in her dreams, he would be wearing even less than that.

The dusky outline of his upper body was sinewy, muscular, but still lean and supple.

"I have been thinking," he said in a low voice, "like you suggested. I think you are right—it *is* better to love and lose, than never to know love at all. For myself, I know only that I do not want to lose you again."

Dallas slowly drew back the covers on the bed. The gesture, and her eyes that burned candle-bright in the dark, invited him in.

His jaw tightened. As Dallas watched, he unfastened his jeans and pulled them down his legs and out from under his feet, and stood naked before her.

He looked very much like the warrior he had been born to be. His legs had the same sinewy grace as his upper body. Wiry, with long, graceful but powerful muscles. A runner's legs.

Dallas found that she couldn't tear her eyes away.

Miguel wasn't modest. Standing naked as his God had made him, he watched as her eyes traveled up and down his body, stopping at the great, jutting thrust of him. Staying there.

After what seemed like an eternity, he came around to the side of the bed.

Reaching, her hands stroked the tight muscles of his stomach, then continued upward and outward in a broad vee to his shoulders. His skin was smooth and hard, not an ounce of superfluous flesh beneath it.

She entwined her arms around his and urged him downward. There was a plea in the gesture that was echoed by her voice. "Please . . ."

"*Querida* . . ." he said in a voice at the same time both rough and tender. "For me, this is not the drop of a hat. . . ."

"Don't say anything. Just come down here."

He did.

Still warm and flushed from sleep, Dallas felt the coolness of his skin through the satiny pajamas she wore. She shivered, whether from the sudden chill or from anticipation, she couldn't have said. She'd never had a man beside her like this, nor even imagined how it might be.

Propped on one elbow, Miguel looked at her the same way she had looked at him—with something resembling awe, as if he had found some rare treasure.

With gentle hands, he smoothed her hair away from her face and fanned it out on the pillow beneath her head. Even in the dim bedroom, it gleamed like fire. The crisp red curls coiled around his fingers, seemed to lick at them like tiny flames consuming kindling wood.

With his other hand he cupped the firm roundness of one breast through the silky, peach-colored pajama top. It was simply made, like a man's shirt; not the yards and yards of cotton and lace Dorthea had worn those nights he'd climbed up the garden trellis and onto the roof of The McAllister's house, just to see her, just to talk to her through the window when the moon and his own forbidden desires kept him from sleep.

But tonight even Dallas's simple clothes were too much. Tonight he wanted her naked. As naked as the Indians when they slept. As naked as he.

Fingers trembling with urgency, he unbuttoned the shirt and pushed the peach-colored fabric away from her body. It caught on his work-roughened hands like the spun-silk skeins of a butterfly's cocoon.

Her skin gleamed milky-white against his own dark flesh. She was the color of an angel, Miguel thought. Together, her bright hair and white skin made her appear surrounded by light. She seemed something to worship, hardly to touch.

But touching was foremost in Miguel's mind. First the firm white breasts revealed by the unbuttoning, then the pink tips, as soft and silky as the pajama top. He rolled them gently between thumb and forefinger, feeling them stiffen and rise beneath his fingertips, as if begging for their touch. Then he bent his head and replaced his fingers with his mouth.

Dallas gasped, a long, shuddering moan that seemed to climb up from deep inside her and escape involuntarily from her throat. It stoked his desire. Abruptly halting the tender teasing of her nipple with his tongue, he sucked it into his mouth with breathtaking intensity.

Again she moaned. Her back arched up from the bed, writhing against him in a paroxysm of pleasure.

Dallas had always thought she'd be awkward the first time, or clumsy, or shy; now she found that she was none of those things. She found that she didn't think at all, only felt, and that the feelings were, as Miguel had assured her, as natural as breathing.

She felt his skin, the tension of all the tiny nerve endings just beneath the surface. She felt an ache in the pit of her stomach, an ache that was a yearning hollowness needing to be filled. She felt his mouth move from one breast to the other, the eager, suckling pressure of his tongue on the underside of her nipple, the slight scraping of teeth on top.

She felt the nerve endings beneath her own skin quiver with tension, too, at all the points of contact between them.

Of their own accord, Dallas felt her hips begin to move against him in the ancient, intuitive rhythms of love. Never having abandoned herself to instinct before, she did so now, without a second's hesitation, trusting Miguel to show her the way.

He reached beneath the elastic waistband of her pajama bottoms and slipped his hand between her legs. His fingers caressed her there, and he found her already moist and ready for him. He tugged the bottoms down, tossed them on the floor, then rolled on top of her, his weight pinning her, a willing prisoner, to the bed.

Rising on a wave of sensation she could neither control nor ignore, Dallas clasped her arms around his neck and pulled him down, meeting his mouth with a ferocity of her own.

Angel or not, Miguel agonized, she was offering herself to him. And he knew that he was no angel. He felt there was a devil inside now, and the devil had to have her. Made him take her.

His hips between her thighs forced them farther apart, demanding that she give more, and more, and more; and she opened herself, straining to give him greater access to her pulsing woman's core.

He reared back, then so quickly that she didn't have time to anticipate the pain, he entered her. A sharp, involuntary cry escaped her lips.

Taken by surprise, Miguel paused momentarily. He moved as though to draw back, but by then the pain was over. By then, her body had accepted him, had accepted the length of him. By then, she felt the thickness of him stroking, with each thrust, the tiny, hidden bud of her sexuality.

The rhythm of their movements changed, began to oppose each other as he plunged downward and she arched upward to meet him, thrust for thrust.

There was pain, but a pain that she savored, craved, *welcomed.* Then she forgot everything she had ever known about pleasure *and* pain, as the exquisite sensation carried her away to a place where no words existed, only sighs and labored breathing, and mindless, urgent cries.

Clasping her arms more tightly around his neck and her legs more tightly around his buttocks, she let the power of his loins carry her up and down and away.

LATER HE WAS GENTLE. He explored her body, memorizing the size, the shape, the feel of her. He held each breast, one at a time, and tasted the nipples, and kissed them with featherlight lips, first the tops and then the soft, white undersides.

"You waited for me, *querida*," he said, his voice full of wonder. "You knew I would come."

"I didn't know what I was waiting for," Dallas whispered. "But I know it now."

FROM THE TOWN SQUARE, recorded Christmas carols repeated monotonously from speakers hidden in the tumbleweed tree. Even in her office with the windows closed, Dallas couldn't get away from them.

Surely they must have more than one tape, she assured herself. But after the third rendition of "I Saw Mommy Kissing Santa Claus," she searched the storeroom in desperation, finally unearthing an old radio she had once seen there. She plugged it in, volume up, in hopes of finding something a little less . . . *commercial.*

There was absolutely nothing going on in the J.P.'s office today.

Even the few cases scheduled didn't show—one of them Dennis the Menace, picked up last night for possession. His long record of misdemeanors had just jumped to felony, Dallas thought with regret but no surprise. *Merry Christmas.*

Was it the approaching holiday? Dallas wondered. Or the impending impeachment petition she knew was circulating the streets? *Must be the petition,* she concluded. Los Reales had never before, in all the years she'd been Justice of the Peace, suspended its lawbreaking proclivities for *any* holiday.

Nothing had changed.

After a night like last night, she'd half expected that *something* would look different, seem different, *be* different.

This morning she had studied the face she saw every morning in the mirror; and except for slight dark rings under the eyes from lack of sleep, it looked pretty much the way it always did.

She had showered, applied makeup and pinned back her hair, as she did every morning,. She had dressed in gray slacks and a turquoise blazer, with a turquoise print blouse and a matching silk scarf knotted on her shoulder, clothes that had been part of her wardrobe for years.

The truck had gone through its usual coughing, choking, gagging routine, as if it, like a human being, needed a dose of caffeine to get started.

The usual people were in the usual places—the crossing guard at the grade school, the sheriff's deputies in the doughnut shop, the storekeepers rolling down their awnings, preparing for the trickle of customers they hoped the day would bring.

The world hadn't changed, but she had, and so had her perception of it. And that made all the difference in the world.

It seemed a more loving place, now that she had found love. It seemed a safer place, where people were misguided, perhaps, but not intentionally mean. The trouble between the de Pimas and the McAllisters was nothing more than a misunderstanding, easily solved—once she and Miguel found a way to help them see it.

She couldn't stop thinking about the strange and wonderful miracle of Miguel's appearance into her life. He was still afraid to trust it, but that was perfectly understandable. What in his previous life had ever taught him to trust?

She had to admit that she had been uncertain, too. But this morning, after a night like last night, she suddenly felt that she had faith enough for both of them. Everything, she was sure, was going to be all right from this day on—with herself, with Miguel, and with Los Reales.

Today there was not the slightest doubt in her mind that if Fate had chosen to return Miguel to this earth, it surely wouldn't be just to let him taste life and love, and then snatch it away again.

Between adjudicating a drop-in case—a minor dispute between the owner of a barking dog and a sleepless neighbor—and collecting several traffic fines, Dallas's mind kept returning to the tragedy that had been Miguel's thirty years on earth.

She couldn't stop thinking about the life he had led, and the man it had made of him.

She knew he must have been an inquisitive and intelligent child, because as a man, he was still that way. She knew he'd gotten as good an education as dedicated Father Sebastiani had been able to provide. She knew he must have been honest, ethical and devout, because he was still very close to his God.

Together, those traits unquestionably would have made him a leader among his people one day, had their lives not been so brutally altered by outside circumstances.

She couldn't stop thinking about Paio. She couldn't stop thinking about the boy.

"Only three days until Christmas," proclaimed an advertisement on the radio. "Don't know what to get your own special Christmas angel...?"

An idea began to take shape in her mind.

It was no more than a what-if sort of idea in the beginning, but it grew and grew and began to take hold of her imagination.

Impossible, she told herself practically, at first, for she was nothing if not practical. *It'd be a miracle.* But the idea kept coming back, and finally it took root in her mind like a seed finding fertile soil. It was worth a try, she finally decided.

After all, miracles certainly seemed to be in the air this Christmas.

Pulling her Rolodex toward her, she began making telephone calls.

AT FIVE O'CLOCK, Dallas set the security alarm, locked the door, and headed for her truck. It was nearly dark, and although the desert always cooled off very quickly after sundown, tonight was colder than usual, even by midwinter standards.

A bitter wind swept through the streets. It threw and by the handfuls against the shop windows. It overturned trash containers and pushed litter ahead of it like flotsom on a tide. Newspapers from a toppled newsstand flapped madly, ready to take wing.

A storm must be coming in, Dallas thought, side-stepping a tumbleweed as big as a small child. Her hair whipped wildly around her head. Wrapping her wool blazer more tightly around her body, she bent into the wind.

But not even the prospect of a storm dampened her spirits tonight. Tonight, even the automated Christmas music emanating from the town square sounded not exactly like a choir of heavenly angels, but cheerful. The lights on the tumbleweed tree twinkled merrily.

It was Christmas, and she was going home. And for the first time since she had left the security of the house where she had grown up, someone would be waiting for her when she got there.

"Heard you had a little trouble out at your place."

Dallas stopped dead in her tracks. She whirled around. The sheriff had exited his office right behind her.

"What do you mean?" she demanded.

Sheriff Cobb bent down to lock his door, then straightened with maddening slowness. "You didn' hear? Yeah, took care of it myself because Mays and Cooper were out on another call—"

"*What happened?*"

"Rock through the window. Big one. Smashed most of the glass clean out. Drove that de Pima fella dow.

to the hardware store to get a plastic tarp and some duct tape to plug up the hole. No clue who did it, of course.

"That de Pima fella said he heard voices yelling and cussing, but by the time he got out to the street, all he saw was a red car rounding the corner on two wheels. Asked him if he got the license number. Acted like he didn't have the first idea what I was talking about—"

"Was he hurt?"

"Who? The de Pima fella? Nah, he wasn't hurt. Few cuts, that's all. Mad as hell, though. Not often I let anybody talk to me like that, especially a de Pima man, but I figured he had a right to be steamed.

"You know, I like you, Dallas, and that fella doesn't seem like such a bad sort, either. But, hey— this kind of thing can't surprise you. Moving a de Pima into your house wasn't the smartest thing you ever did—hey, where're you going?"

By the time he'd gotten the words out of his mouth, Dallas was halfway down the block.

Upon reaching her truck, she jerked open the door, then slammed it shut behind her and squealed out of the parking lot in a flurry of small stones.

Her disjointed thoughts buzzed around inside her head like killer bees zeroing in on her brain. *I was so sure it was over.* Hot tears blurred her vision. *I was so sure! What made me think that? Whatever made me think that one night of love between two insignificant mortals mattered at all?*

She felt like a fool for expecting more. A buffoon of cosmos proportions. Somewhere high overhead, she was sure she heard God laughing.

Arriving at the Gulf Winds Condominium Complex, she ground the gearshift into park, and leapt from the truck.

The storm had grown stronger. It bent the palm trees almost double, and lashed the air with their fronds. Sand, whipped to a frenzy by the wind, stung her face and hands like needles.

Dallas fought the gusts that threatened to sweep her off her feet, and struggled up the sidewalk. Her progress was measured in inches.

At last she made it to the front door.

"Miguel!" she screamed, pounding on it as if to break it down. "Miguel!" When he opened it, she threw herself, sobbing, into his arms.

He swept her inside, then slammed the door shut against the storm that was trying to force its way into the house. He held her tightly, trying to calm her.

"What has happened, *querida?*" he demanded in an alarmed voice.

"Sheriff Cobb...told me...the rock..." she hiccuped brokenly against the hard wall of his chest.

"Is that all?" Miguel exclaimed, relieved. "It was nothing. Nothing! I am not hurt."

He *was* hurt. "A few cuts," Sheriff Cobb had said. Dallas herself had seen a gash on his cheek the minute he'd opened the door. But it was neither the sheriff's information, nor the rock, nor the admittedly minor injuries that had brought her to the edge of hysteria.

It was the excruciating knowledge that love, after all, hadn't changed a thing.

Chapter Fourteen

Shortly after midnight on Christmas Eve, it began to snow. There were only a few delicate, sporadic flurries, catching in the spines of the saguaros and glittering in the moonlight like bits of a fallen star.

Later, Dallas roused to see snowflakes drifting like a curtain of lace past her bedroom window. Cocooned in that hazy twilight world between waking and sleeping, she smiled sleepily and snuggled closer to Miguel.

"It's going to be a white Christmas," she murmured.

Miguel opened his eyes a slit. Still snowing, he noted vaguely, only half awake. Then he remembered, and his eyes flew open.

Not *still* snowing, he thought, an icy feeling of dread stealing over him.

Snowing *again*.

Moving slowly so as not to disturb Dallas, he slipped from beneath the blankets. Avoiding, as he had very quickly learned to do, the full-length mirror on the closet door, he moved as silently as a ghost to the window.

He saw that the snowflakes vanished as soon as they touched the desert floor, but looking toward the foothills of the Huachucas, he could see that they had already begun to dust the rocky ledges.

The feeling of dread deepened. It never snowed in the desert. In the high mountain valleys, yes, and occasionally a dusting in the foothills. But not on the desert floor, never on the desert floor. Not quite *never,* the dread in his heart forced him to remember. *Once.*

Fear cut through him like a blade.

It was happening again! Dallas had been too quick to believe; *he* had been too willing to hope.

Now, when his life and his love had somehow been returned to him, he was going to lose them again, just as he had one hundred years ago. And he was as powerless now as he had been then.

Maybe even more so. The last time, right up to the instant The McAllister had fired his rifle, Miguel had harbored that most basic of human instincts—the visceral denial of his own ceasing to be. This couldn't really be happening—not to him, not to Dorthea, not to the love they had believed was immortal. Someone had made a mistake.

But it had happened. And it looked like it was going to happen again.

And this time, there was no basic human instinct on which he could hang a hope; now he knew with clear-eyed certainty that the God of Father Sebastiani, despite the old priest's simple faith, was indifferent to the lives of men.

My God, he raged inwardly, determined to batter his way through that indifference. *Tell me what to do! I have done everything I can think of—what more is expected of me?*

But there was no reply in the dark world beyond the window. No message written across the sky, no words of wisdom echoing down from the mountains. Not even any feeling within Miguel's heart that anyone had heard his plea. There was only the night, and the moon shadows on the desert, and the silent, falling, relentless snow.

With a knot in his gut that twisted more tightly every second, Miguel returned to bed. He slipped one arm beneath Dallas's head and pulled her close, and buried his face in her hair. His eyes stared bleakly into the darkness.

"Br-r-r, you're so cold," she grumbled, flinging one arm across his chest. "Here—" she snuggled closer "—let me warm you."

Despite the turbulent emotions churning deep within him, and the chill that came from somewhere deeper still, Miguel felt his body respond.

She was soft beside him, only half awake. The arm she had thrown across his chest ventured lower, and her fingers fit themselves around his rising masculinity.

"Yes, *querida,* warm me," he echoed.

Still heavy-lidded, whether from sleep or from something more, Miguel wasn't sure, Dallas rose up on one elbow.

As she leaned down to kiss him and to trace his lips with the tip of her tongue, her perfect breasts plumped gently on his chest. Their peaks were already hard with passion. He tried to cup one in his palm, but the firm tips moved out of his reach and skimmed tantalizingly down his chest and stomach, following the path her hand had taken.

Rising to her knees, Dallas curved herself over him. Still holding his throbbing length in her hand, she brushed her taut nipples back and forth across him, first one, then the other, until Miguel groaned like an animal into the darkness.

"Let me have you," he begged in a hoarse voice that sounded not at all like his own. "Now."

Was it a blessing or a curse, he asked himself in an agony of desire, that even while the fate of his immortal soul hung in the balance, he could still want her this much?

"Not quite yet," she whispered.

The words and her warm breath tickled Miguel's sensitive, straining flesh, and his entire body tightened like a coiled spring. Where his hands had been splayed, fingers digging into the mattress, they now balled into fists, clenching and unclenching with almost superhuman effort, resisting the ecstasy that threatened to overwhelm him.

His flexed buttocks forced his hips upward, closer to her, and with the mouth and lips that could be as soft and yielding as silk, she did things to him for which he didn't even have a name.

It was a pleasure-that-was-almost-pain, rooted at the very core of his passion, and rushing like a thousand tiny cactus spines to every nerve ending in his body. At the juncture of his thighs, his hands had entangled themselves in Dallas's fiery hair.

"Now!" he gritted through clenched teeth, and there was a command in his voice that Dallas could no longer ignore.

Releasing her hold on him, she undulated upward, caressing his body with hers, an inch at a time, until they were face-to-face. Then, stretched out on top, she parted her thighs and let her knees slide down on either side of his hips. Straddling him, open and ready and needing, she let him come in. With the first thrust, she caught her breath, then she began to breath in unison with his rhythm, inhaling with a gasp at each deep thrust, exhaling with a shuddering, involuntary moan at each withdrawal.

Damp skin moved against damp skin, muscle against muscle, hard, urgent flesh inside receptive softness, and Dallas knew it all, felt it all, wanted it all.

Her gasps and moans came faster and faster with his increasing tempo, until at last her breath was so labored that she felt as though she couldn't get enough air into her lungs, and her entire body begged for release. Then suddenly he clasped her hips and held them down, at the same time burying himself to the hilt inside her.

She cried out, then caught her breath and held it while the spasms of her own body contracted around him.

Then she felt him open her even more. He gripped her buttocks with hard hands to anchor her against him, then thrust himself savagely upward and exploded into her.

In the world beyond the bedroom window, the snow kept falling. Softly. Steadily. Inexorably. When morning came, the hills were white. The snow lay as fine as sprinkled salt on the desert sand.

When Dallas woke, she was surprised. Snow in the foothills, yes. That happened once or twice every winter, softening the winter barrenness of the jagged rocks. But snow on the desert floor? A few old-timers remembered a time or two when that had happened, but Dallas had never in her life seen it. It put her in mind of the writings of Father Sebastiani—*snow...no one alive remembered such snow.*

Donning a pair of jeans and a bulky, vanilla-colored cable-knit sweater, she shivered uneasily.

MIGUEL was also shivering.

Seated on a stool at Dallas's tiny breakfast bar, he couldn't remember when he had ever been so cold.

Not even in Dallas's home, with what she called central heat, could he seem to get warm.

Even after the hearty breakfast they had prepared together, which should certainly have warmed him from the inside out, he was still cold.

"More coffee?" Dallas asked. Miguel nodded, but when she brought it to him, he didn't drink it. Instead he wrapped his hands around the steaming cup and held it, as he had the first two, until he had absorbed most of the coffee's heat into his icy hands.

The shivering tension that racked his body worried Dallas. The thermostat was set at nearly eighty degrees, and she felt as though she was in a sauna, and still he shivered.

Was it just the unaccustomed snow? she wondered. Or might he have caught a virus of some sort? Who knew if his immune system could handle viruses and other illness-causing bugs that hadn't even existed one hundred years ago?

Or could he be getting ready to... leave? To return to that cold nothingness that was the only thing he remembered? Dallas felt panic tightening her chest.

For a time, a very *short* time, it seemed to her now—right after they had first made love and it seemed nothing could disturb their perfect joy—she had been sure that everything was going to turn out all right.

Miguel was part of her now, and she part of him; how could anything come between them?

But against her will, a niggling doubt in the back of her mind forced Dallas to acknowledge that the love he had held for Dorthea, and she for him, a love so strong that it had lasted more than one hundred years, hadn't been enough to keep them together. What guarantee did she have that this time would be any different? She tried not to think about that.

And then that rock had come through the window.

It had shattered more than the front window. It had also shattered the dream world Dallas had constructed for herself and Miguel. Her dream was not extravagant, only a future together, a home and children, far from Los Reales and its stupid feud mentality, and free from the directives of a God with His own, indecipherable agenda.

The rock through the window had made her understand that something was still expected of Miguel, although it was now as much a mystery as it had been the first night he had arrived here.

"There must be something we should be doing," Dallas exclaimed vehemently. Seated across from Miguel at the breakfast bar, her frustration and her fear were palpable. "There's *got* to be *some*thing we're overlooking!"

"I fear I have done enough already," Miguel replied somberly, hands still wrapped around the warm coffee cup. "I have put innocent lives, including your own, in danger. The town is more dangerous than it was before I came. The only thing left to do is to give a battle cry and let Los Reales wipe itself from the face of the earth."

Dallas reached across the breakfast bar to squeeze his arm. "Do you really believe you've been sent forward in time just to destroy Los Reales? I don't think so."

She smiled grimly. "There *is* something else—there *has* to be. It's just a matter of finding it."

"And finding it in time," Miguel added.

He lifted the coffee abruptly to his lips and drained the cup in one long swallow. He felt the warmth all the way down his throat and into his belly, where it immediately began to cool. "But we know nothing— nothing! We don't even know if this whole business truly *is* God's work."

His voice fell to a reluctant whisper. "We don't even know if the God of Father Sebastiani really even *exists.*"

He paused, half expecting some terrible retribution for his blasphemy, or at least to feel Father Sebastiani's hard wooden ruler smacking down on his knuckles. But there was nothing. More evidence, to Miguel's tormented mind, of His indifference, or else His nonexistence. Since the result was the same, it hardly mattered which.

"Hush, Miguel," Dallas remonstrated urgently. "Don't say that. Don't even think it."

Standing, she turned the thermostat up two more degrees, then hooked her thumbs into the back pockets of her jeans and walked to the patio door. Through it, she had a panoramic view of the dun-colored desert floor with its salt-sprinkle of white growing thicker, the snow-dusted Huachuca foothills, and the lowering gray shell of the sky.

It was an uninspiring scene.

"Don't forget Father Sebastiani said 'forgiveness,' too," she reminded him. "That's got to mean something."

On the surface, Dallas thought the old friar's words had an encouraging ring to them. But try though she did, taking the words apart and rearranging them in every possible permutation, she still couldn't come up with any combination that told them what was expected of them.

Suddenly Dallas whirled around. "Miguel, there *is* one possibility. I don't know why I didn't think of it before. My father."

"Your father?" He sounded dubious.

"Yes. Maybe the McAllister point of view might have some bearing on the outcome of the story. If my father can tell us anything about the McAllister version of the story that's different from what Father Sebastiani wrote, we might find something important that we're overlooking. Maybe we'll find some detail we might be missing."

"Do you believe your father knows anything about what happened?"

"It's not an official part of McAllister history, no. Not the way it is of Papago legends. *I* had never heard much about it until we began searching. But if there's any McAllister version of it at all, my father will know it."

Miguel still looked doubtful. "What makes you think your father would be willing to help me?"

"He probably won't be," Dallas admitted frankly. "But I think he might be willing to help *me*."

Coming face-to-face with Dallas's father would not have been Miguel's first choice of a way to spend what might very well prove to be his last day on earth. But if she thought it might give them something more to go on, he agreed to try.

Still, her hope-filled words had significantly different connotations to him.

Her father.

The head of the McAllister Clan.

The McAllister.

To him, they sounded like a death knell.

"WHAT'ER YE DOING galavantin' around in the middle of the day? Why ain't cha workin'?" Rooster grumbled in his chronically disgruntled voice from the depths of his easy chair.

"It's Christmas Eve, Pa. The office is closed for the holidays."

His eyes didn't deviate from his black-and-white television screen until the commercials came on. Then he turned toward Dallas and, in doing so, caught sight of Miguel right beside her.

Disbelieving, his eyes shot from one face to the other, then returned in a paroxysm of outrage to hers.

"Pa, this is—"

"I know full well who it is, Dorothy Alice!" The old man choked on his words. "Now get him outta here!"

Practically apoplectic, he thumped his cane on the floor while he sputtered for breath, then struggled to haul himself to his feet. "No thievin' de Pima ever set foot across this threshold since the old judge built this place, and I ain't gonna have it be startin' now."

He raised the cane in the air as if to swing it, then instead jabbed the tip like a sword against Miguel's chest.

"Out! Out!" he bellowed with each jab. And with each jab, Miguel retreated, one step at a time, closer to the door. "G'wan, get outta here!"

Except for his bristling shock of red hair, the man didn't really look much like The McAllister; Miguel thought. He was shorter and stouter, without the arrogant presence that had allowed The McAllister to command the entire town from atop his black stallion.

The blood had thinned, Miguel thought; but it had resurfaced in Dallas. She looked more like The McAllister than she did her own father. But in her courage, her independence, her kindness, she resembled no one so much as Dorthea.

Dorthea.

Upon entering the old McAllister house, the first thing he had seen was the daguerreotype of Dorthea hanging in the hallway. To come across her face so unexpectedly gave him something of a shock, and for an instant it filled him with pain as fresh as if it had not occurred one hundred years ago.

The likeness must have been made about the time he had first come to work for The McAllister, for it still had the slight girlishness he remembered from the first time he'd ever seen her.

The second year, her face had matured, revealing the fine-boned beauty that would no doubt be part of her all her life. The second year, she had looked exactly like Dallas.

It pleased Miguel to think that Dallas was the kind of woman Dorthea might have become. It also pleased him to think that, in some way not easily explained, she could experience through Dallas a life freer than the one she had known.

Retreating one step at a time, suddenly Miguel felt the wall at his back. He caught the tip of the old man's cane mid-jab.

"Enough," he said brusquely. It was a tone Dallas had never yet heard from him, and she glanced in his direction, startled. His no-nonsense voice carried more authority than all of Rooster's blustering.

Still holding the tip of the cane in his hand as a barrier between himself and the old man, with Rooster jerking futilely on the other end to pull it free, Miguel leveled a questioning look toward Dallas. "Shall I wait outside? It is, after all, his house."

"Damn de Pima's got more sense'n you do, girl," Rooster interrupted his litany of imprecations to concur fiercely. "Now get out, the both o' you!"

"Pa, Miguel's not leaving, and neither am I. Now just sit down—" she gestured to Miguel, who released his hold on the cane and let its tip drop to the floor ''—and stop that carrying on. There are a few things I want to ask you about the family, and then we'll be on our way.''

Pointedly ignoring Miguel, the old man stumped back to his chair and fell heavily into it. He propped his cane between his knees, folded his hands on the crooked wooden handle, and looked up at Dallas malevolently. ''Go ahead, ask, if'n you want. I ain't promisin' I'm gonna tell you nothin'.''

''Pa, I need to know...'' Dallas began, then stopped.

She wasn't sure where to begin. Suddenly she realized how little her taciturn father had ever spoken about the history of the McAllisters in this region. Was that because there wasn't much to tell? Or was it secrets?

''I need to know about the McAllisters, Pa,'' she continued. ''I need to know where we fit into this feud business—''

''Might'a known!'' Rooster snorted. ''We don't fit into the feud at all! Feud's got nothin' to do with McAllisters! It's them de Pimas. They're *all* bad. *Allus* been bad, ever since the first settlers came here. They found these Mexican papists and a lazy bunch of Indians squattin' on prime land, not doing nothin' with it. So naturally they took it.

''But those de Pima Indians fought 'em every step o' the way—it ain't no wonder a blood feud started up! But it wadn't McAllisters started it—it was *them*, those shiftless, no-count de Pimas.''

"So that's how you think the feud got started, Pa? Long before the McAllisters got here? Is there anything else you can tell me about it, or about how it began?''

"*Me?* Not *me*, girl. I may be old, but I ain't as old as God! Feud's got nothing to do with McAllisters. We was just the ones were here when the Indians decided to go on the warpath, that's all.''

"But that happened all over the Tucson Valley, Pa. Everywhere else people got past it. Why not us? Why not Los Reales?''

"Them de Pimas was a mean bunch. Right from the get-go, they wouldn't go along with nothin'. Not new crops, not the cattle. Not even the copper minin', and hell, that coulda made 'em rich! We could *all*'a been rich!—steada suckin' hind tit like we do. It's their fault, them de Pima bastids. Right from the get-go, they was a mean bunch.''

"But Miguel says he remem—that there was a time when there was no feud.''

"*Oh, Mee-gel sez*, does he?'' Rooster mimicked in a mincing imitation of a feminine voice. "Well, what does a goddamn de Pima know, anyway? Specially when he ain't been in town more'n two weeks, and 'specially when he's been causin' trouble since the day he showed up?''

"I intended to cause no trouble,'' Miguel interjected with cold courtesy. "I only meant to live here.''

"*Live* here?" Rooster shifted his malevolent eyes to Miguel and snorted contemptuously. "*Live* here, you say, de Pima? Didn't wanna cause no trouble, you say? Well, then, mebbe you shoulda stayed on your own side o'town insteada movin' in at my daughter's place."

Dallas reddened. She raised one hand to her forehead to shield her embarrassment. How had he found out so quickly? "Pa!" she exclaimed angrily.

"Mebbe you shoulda found one o' your own women," Rooster continued as if she hadn't spoken, "insteada you an' my Dorothy Alice prancin' around on Main Street like you owned it, huh?"

Rooster's faded blue eyes glittered triumphantly. "Ja ever think about *that*, Mr. Don't Wanna Cause No Trouble?"

Miguel moved from the shadows of the doorway into the light. "I moved into your daughter's home because I believed she needed protection. I still believe so."

"What kind o' protection does my girl need from the likes o' you?" Rooster scoffed.

"I feel the need to protect her from those who would hurt her. And from having her tires slashed, and rocks thrown through her window—"

"And from being accosted in a parking lot by a bunch of local thugs." She turned aside to tell him in a low voice. "I didn't mention it to you, Miguel, I didn't know what you'd do."

Already the tightening of his features and his fists made her glad she hadn't mentioned the incident at the time.

Rooster looked at Dallas, too, his own face rigid. "Did someone lay their hands on you, girl?" he asked grimly. "If they did, they're gonna pay. They're gonna pay—"

"No, Pa, no one touched me." But if Tom Mays hadn't pulled up when he had... She shuddered, remembering.

Rooster sagged back in his chair. He looked deflated, as if all the fight had been let out of him, like air out of a balloon. "Dorothy Alice, believe me when I tell you I didn't know nothin' about this. If I'da had, I'da put a stop to it right away, I shorely would."

"Pa, it's all connected to the feud. You've been part of it so long a little violence shouldn't surprise you."

"Not against me an' mine," the old man mumbled wretchedly. "Not against my own daughter."

Dallas was surprised. Had he ever been like this before? she wondered. So worried about her, as if he really cared? When he was a young man, maybe, or when her mother left? If so, she had never seen it. By the time she was old enough to realize that fathers were people, too, he was the curmudgeon he had been ever since.

Suddenly Rooster sat up straighter. "I want you t'come home, Dorothy Alice," he announced, his jaw as set as a bulldog's. "Nobody'll bother you out here. You come stay until this whole thing blows over—"

"Exactly what makes you think it's going to blow over, Pa?"

Rooster jerked his head in Miguel's direction. "Once *he* moves on, everything'll be back to the way they was. There've been flare-ups like this before. You'll see, people'll forget. They allus do." Rooster looked at her almost pleadingly. "Come home, girl. I don't want t'see nothin' happen t'you."

She wanted to tell him that Miguel wasn't moving on. She wanted to tell him that Miguel was here to stay. But of course, she couldn't.

"I'm sorry, Pa," she replied as gently as she could. "I can't. I have a job to do in town."

"What job?" Rooster sputtered, already back in character. "It's Christmas Eve—you already said you ain't gonna keep your office open on Christmas Eve!"

"Not that job, Pa. Look, Pa, talk to me about the feud, okay? Are there any family stories you might have heard at one time or another? Something no one else might know?"

Rooster glared at her suspiciously. "Like what?"

"Oh, say like the Indian myth about a McAllister woman and a de Pima man falling in love, and the man being chased down and hung on Christmas Eve? Do we have any stories like that?"

"Pack o' lies!" the old man sputtered again, thumping his cane furiously on the floor for emphasis. "The old judge never hung no one what wadn't a thief or a murderer, or some kinda outlaw!"

"Tell me about the hanging, Pa."

"The hangin' had nothin' to do with it. It was some crazy old papist said that, and the Indians believed him. But it wadn't true, none o' it. The man they hung was a horse thief, or some kinda criminal, anyways, else the judge wouldn't never've done it like that, with no trial nor nothin'.

"Him an' his posse'd tracked the man for days, and they finally caught up with him at the old San Xavier Mission. He tried to hide out behind the priest's skirts, but they dragged him out and they hung him."

Rooster's voice had trailed to a monotone. He looked up at Dallas defensively. "Twadn't legal, exactly, from the way I heard when I was a boy. But it *was* justice, all the same. It was the law of the Old West—you couldn't let a man get away with horse stealing. A lotta good men died, by Indians or by thirst or by their own hand when the sun scrambled their brains, because some horse thief stole their horse and left 'em stranded out there in the middle of the desert."

"The man was not a horse thief." Miguel spoke out suddenly in a voice as sepulchral as a tomb. But Dallas and Rooster looked at him in surprise. "The McAllister murdered him for one reason only—to keep him from marrying his daughter."

Rooster's faded blue eyes grew wide. "What did you say?"

"The man they hung was not a horse thief, no matter what The McAllister claimed. The McAllister hung him to prevent—"

"The McAllister," Rooster echoed. "You said *The McAllister.* How'd you know that name? Nobody called him that—not after he got appointed territorial judge, at least. From then on he wouldn't allow it. *How'd you know that name?"*

Miguel backpedaled furiously. "I must have heard it someplace, just as you did."

"No," said Rooster slowly. "I never heard it. I read it in some old family papers I found in my granddaddy's stuff when he died. I never heard nobody say *The McAllister* like that 'cepting you."

Rooster stared up at Miguel strangely. "Who *are* you?" he croaked in a whisper.

Chapter Fifteen

"Well, that was pretty much a waste of time," Dallas remarked, guiding her truck down the slick highway back to town. "My father knows even less about the feud than we do."

She leaned forward to peer intently through the windshield that the wiper blades could barely clear. "I've never seen so much snow," she worried under her breath.

Flipping on the radio, she scanned the Tucson stations, hearing snatches of Christmas carols sung by everyone from the Mormon Tabernacle Choir to Willie Nelson, but not a single weather report about the extraordinary snowfall in Los Reales.

"It was not altogether a waste of time," Miguel countered. "We did learn a few things. What your father said goes along with what Father Sebastiani wrote—it is just that the McAllisters do not believe the murder had anything to do with the feud. That means we are probably right in thinking Christmas Eve is—"

"The deadline," Dallas interrupted, a catch in her throat. "It means we were right in thinking that today is probably the...last—our last...."

Miguel took one of her hands from the wheel and clasped it between his own. "Maybe. Maybe not. The day is not over yet." He raised her hand to his lips and kissed it.

The words were intended to bolster Dallas's spirits, but deep inside himself, Miguel felt as disheartened as she.

What, he wondered hopelessly, could he do in twelve hours that he had not been able to accomplish in nearly two weeks?

The lacy veil of snow continued to fall, as if with some impenetrable purpose of its own. Against that blazing whiteness, Dallas's coppery hair was a contrast achingly familiar.

Again, he thought in despair. *Again?*

He scrutinized her profile, framed by a riot of red curls. The resolute set of her lips squared her jaw into a very good imitation of her father's bulldog expression. It told Miguel how determined she was to find the solution to this mystery.

She would battle with God Himself, he thought, half in admiration, half in fear.

But the teardrops he saw trembling on her lower lashes told him that she was also very, very afraid.

"Querida mia," he said softly. "Let us go home."

The tears dropped and coursed crookedly down her cheeks. She brushed them away with impatient fingers. "You're . . . giving up," she accused him brokenly.

"No, I am not. But I do want to go home with you. If God wants me, He will know where to find me."

A LAYER OF SNOW made the secondary roads almost impassable. Dallas had to keep the truck in four-wheel drive and creep along at a snail's pace.

Main Street, when she finally reached it, was also impassable, although not with snow, because the traffic of last-minute Christmas shopping had turned much of it to slush. Instead, Main Street was blocked with vehicles of every description, all parked helter-skelter as if their drivers had simply abandoned them in the middle of the road.

Dallas tsk-tsked wryly. "No one around here knows anything about driving in snow. The sheriff's department would be having a field day out here—*if* they could get their *own* cruisers out of the garage!"

Upon closer inspection, it also appeared that the drivers of the abandoned vehicles, as much as half the population of Los Reales—the north-side half—were assembled in the town square, in front of the snow-laden tumbleweed Christmas tree.

"What in the world is going on?" Dallas wondered aloud.

"Looks like a mob to me," Miguel said uneasily. *Again*, the thought flashed through his mind. *Again!*

His trepidation transferred itself to Dallas, and her pulse began to quicken. "Let me go check it out," she said casually, trying to inject a note of nonchalance into her voice.

Turning to Miguel, she kissed him quickly. "I'll be right back. But if...if anything happens that looks the least bit...*unusual,* you turn this truck around and drive like a bat out of hell for Tucson. You remember the way?"

"Of course."

She turned her leather handbag upside down. "You'll need money," she said, shoving into his hand all the bills in her wallet.

"Dallas, no! I will not let you do this!" Miguel moved to open the door on his side of the truck. "I will not leave you!"

"Miguel, these are my people—they're not going to hurt me, not really. Threaten me a little because they're in a fighting mood, maybe, but it's not me they're after—it's you! Please, just trust me!"

Fiercely she wound her arms around his neck and pulled him close. "I love you," she whispered. "I've always loved you."

With that, she jumped from the driver's seat and began to wade through the ankle-deep slush.

MIGUEL WATCHED her slosh awkwardly toward the town square. She was so small, so brave, marching like David with his slingshot into combat with Goliath— one of Father Sebastiani's stories, and one Miguel desperately hoped was true.

When she reached the edge of the crowd, she skirted it on tiptoe, trying to see over the heads of the people, searching for an opening. Suddenly she spied one. Squeezing herself between two bulky gray parkas, the crush of people folded around her and she vanished.

The crowd seemed agitated.

At the front, Miguel could see the head and shoulders of one man taller than the rest. Obviously standing on a bench or on the hood of a vehicle of some kind, he was shouting at the mob, waving his arms in the air as if to incite them to some kind of action.

Miguel waited restively, continuously scanning for Dallas among the throng. She was nowhere to be seen. Time passed at a snail's pace. Glancing at the dashboard clock, he saw that she had been gone for all of ten minutes—it seemed like hours.

Suddenly a red pickup with yellow flames painted on its fenders, and gigantic, oversize tires, came careening up Main Street. Its driver deftly maneuvered around the crazily parked cars, then angled into the minuscule space between Dallas's truck and the van parked crosswise in front of it. The driver jumped out and hurried away.

The pickup blocked Miguel's view of the square, but peering out the side window, he saw several men carting equipment out of the hardware store.

Ladders. Shovels. Eventually the driver of the pickup—it was the rancher whom Dallas had called Wyatt Slocum—strode out of the store with a thick length of rope looped around one shoulder.

Beads of sweat broke out on Miguel's forehead. *Madre de Dios,* he prayed inwardly. *Protect me!* He hit the floor and crouched there like a hunted animal, his heart pounding hammerlike against his ribs.

He was cold again, colder than before, and the chill went clear to his bones. He blew on his hands and rubbed the palms together, but the resulting friction did nothing to warm him. *It is my life,* he thought fearfully, *preparing to leave my body.*

If only he could see! Miguel groaned from the dimness of the floorboards. Where was Dallas? What was taking so long? Then another possibility struck him.

What if she *couldn't* come back? What if they had imprisoned her, in hopes that she might lead them to him?

That was what The McAllister had done to Dorthea. But he had never expected that his daughter, headstrong though she was, would dare disobey him by climbing out the window and down the rose trellis. He hadn't suspected how much practice Dorthea had had in doing exactly that.

The red pickup rumbled to life, vibrating the very air around it as it drove away. But not until he could no longer hear its engine even faintly in the distance did Miguel crawl out of his hiding place, and then it was only to peer furtively over the dashboard, hoping to catch a glimpse of Dallas.

While surveying the crowd, Miguel realized suddenly that it was beginning to break apart. Moving quickly, people returned to the cars and trucks they had abandoned. Their movements appeared single-minded and purposeful.

Watching, he saw that they spoke little, and the expressions on their faces were grim.

Miguel had seen faces like that before. He knew what a mob looked like, whether on horseback or in trucks and cars. He knew what a mob sounded like. And he knew from bitter, firsthand knowledge how quickly a mob could lose control.

Dallas had asked him to trust her. She had said her own people would not hurt her.

But they had already hurt her.

The slashing of her tires was undoubtedly a de Pima trick. But the rock through her window? And what about the assault in the parking lot? Those were her own people, and they were every bit as vicious to one of their own as they would be to a de Pima from a hundred years ago, who wanted nothing to do with their feud.

His survival instincts took over.

With shaking fingers, he turned the key in the ignition and threw the truck into gear. Gunning the engine like a race car driver, he made a hairpin U-turn in the middle of the street, fishtailing wildly in the slushy snow, and headed straight for the highway that led to Tucson.

BUT HE NEVER intended to go to Tucson. He could not go that far away from Dallas.

Even if he somehow managed to escape with his life, it would be worth nothing without her.

No, he was not going to Tucson. Instead he pulled off the highway onto the road that led to the White Dove of the Desert. In the distance, the Mission looked exactly as it always had, glowing whitely in the middle of the plain of desert.

It occurred to him vaguely that this was the last place he should be going on Christmas Eve, with a mob not far behind him—but he was running on instinct now, and there seemed nowhere else to go.

Time distorted in his mind. He knew what day it was—*but what year?*

Listening for horses' hooves behind him, his breath came faster, as if the truck were running on his strength alone, on his effort. It took every ounce of his physical strength to keep the truck moving, to keep himself running.

The Mission, when at last he veered into its parking lot, was dark. The only light was the little that was left of the day and the cold eye of the winter moon, peering indistinctly through low-riding gray clouds. It gave the white adobe a hazy, unearthly quality that added to Miguel's rising fear.

Except for a few tire tracks in the parking lot, already disappearing under a layer of new snow, there was no sign of life at all.

The parking lot should have been lined with *luminarias*. The portal should have been opened wide. The altar should have been ablaze with candles, making the church shine like a beacon far into the desert.

And there should be children. It was the final night of *Las Posadas,* and the children should have been at their gayest in the *posadas* procession, bearing candles, singing, carrying Baby Jesus to his straw-filled manger to be born.

More and more disquieted, Miguel drove around back and pulled the truck into the old carriage house where Father Kino stored the garden tools. At least it would not reveal his presence if anyone came looking for him.

Trying the kitchen door and finding it open, he slipped inside. His mind was a confusion of time and space, and he felt as though someone else was somehow directing his every movement.

He tried to turn on a light, but found that the switch on the wall did nothing. In the darkness of the Mission's interior, he made his way through the maze of thick adobe walls to the sacristy, and from there into the church.

The high clerestory windows were filled with gray evening. A suggestion of moonlight flowed through them, picking up the pigments of the stained glass and projecting them onto the tiled floor in prisms of muted colors.

The church had a musky odor—a pungent combination of the humanity that had passed between its walls over the centuries, wax burned from thousands of candles, and time. The smell was hauntingly familiar, a memory from his earliest years, when the same smell had made him feel safe in God's hands.

The niches and domed ceilings of the old church were filled with the breath of a million prayers. Dropping to his knees before the crucifix on the altar, Miguel sent his own up to join them.

Suddenly he became aware of a sound impinging on the edges of his consciousness. Not horses' hooves, at least, but growing louder, changing from one sound to many, and building to a cacophony like a choir of demons growling in the parking lot.

Engines, Miguel remembered in panic. *Trucks. Cars.* The motorized vehicles he had believed to be miracles. Now he understood that they were no miracle, but instruments of the Devil. They had made it possible for the mob to find him much sooner than he ever would have believed.

Doors slammed. Voices shouted. The sounds of the mob came closer, were right outside the portal.

Miguel leapt to his feet. His mind was suddenly crystal-clear, and he stared in disbelief at his surroundings.

Fool that I am, he berated himself. *What am I doing here? There is no safety for me here. There never was!*

He didn't even consider running. There was nowhere to run, he knew that.

Life was a circle, he thought despairingly, and he had come around again, nothing more than a puppet in some insane play God had created for His own amusement.

The outcome had already been decided, and there was nothing for Miguel to do but wait powerlessly for his fate to be fulfilled.

He felt betrayed. "Not again," he protested in agony, feeling farther from God than the tides of eternity Father Sebastiani had spoke of so often.

The words ascended toward the frescoed ceilings grayed with the smoke of a million votive candles, where they joined the centuries of prayers already hovering there.

But when they echoed back through the silence of the old church, it was only the last word that remained audible. ...*again!*

If only he might be allowed to see Dallas once more, to know that she was safe!

Then, he vowed, he would give himself up to the mob, and let them do with him what they would. His death—whether by hanging or by whatever means they chose in this strange, new world—would add more fuel to their feud, would allow it to continue for another hundred years.

Suddenly he heard a drove of footsteps just outside the portal. Then he heard the scrape of the key in the lock.

Not even aware that he did so, Miguel backed toward the crucifix that hung over the altar.

Chapter Sixteen

"Miguel!"

In the gray twilight, with only faint moonlight filtering through the high windows, Dallas saw him, and she ran down the aisle to him.

"Dallas!" Oblivious to the mob behind her, Miguel vaulted over the communion rail and met her at the bottom of the tiled steps. He reached out to clasp her in his arms at the same time that she threw herself into them.

"Oh, Miguel," she cried, her arms tight around his waist, her face pressed against his chest. "When I came back and the truck was gone—I *knew* what happened! I knew what you must have thought!"

He buried his face in her damp, tangled hair. He said nothing, only held her as if to take her breath away. The sight of her, the feel of her, vital and alive in his arms, was enough.

He'd made a bargain with God, and God, for His own capricious reasons, had chosen to honor it. Soon it would be Miguel's turn to ante up; but now, he gave himself over to the moment. He was fully a man, he was fully alive, and for now nothing else mattered.

"Oh, Miguel, how you must have felt! I was afraid you'd gone to Tucson." Her voice was muffled against his chest. "I was afraid I wouldn't be able to find you! I was so scared!"

Miguel rubbed his cheek back and forth over her damp hair. "I know, *querida mia*," he whispered fervently. "So was I. But you should have known I would never have left you."

"Miguel, my son," a familiar voice hailed him from the vestibule. He looked up to see Father Kino striding up the aisle, his brown cassock flapping at his feet to reveal very secular boots and blue jeans.

The priest slapped him on the back. "I should have known I'd find you here! We have more than enough equipment—go find yourself a shovel and get to work! Just let me go change this—" he shrugged out of the cassock, which he had been in the process of unbuttoning "—for something easier to move in, and I'll join you outside."

He winked like a coconspirator as he hurried away. "God works in mysterious ways."

Miguel looked down at Dallas, total bewilderment in his eyes. "What does he mean? Why have all these people come here?"

"It's okay. Everything's all right." She tilted her face up to him, and even in the dim light, her white skin glistened, covered with a fine sheen of melted snow and tears.

"It's the Mission. It's the snow," she told him. "It's the weight of the snow, actually—isn't it amazing how much those tiny little flakes can add up?—and of course, no one can even remember when it snowed like this before—"

Her eager voice tripped over itself, but Miguel quickly caught the crux of what she was trying to say. She was here. She was smiling. If she said everything was all right, he thought incredulously, it *must* be.

There was no lynch mob.

There never had been.

"I thought..." he began.

"I *know* what you thought. For a crazy instant, I thought it, too.... But it wasn't! It was only Father Kino! The roof over the church is collapsing from the snow. And the telephone lines are down, so he had to come all the way into town to get help. And look, Miguel—*look!*" She made a sweeping gesture that took in the entire room.

He looked, but all he saw were men and women rushing into and out of the church, carrying ladders and ropes and lengths of metal and two-by-fours.

"Don't you see?" Dallas persisted.

Suddenly he did.

Folks recognizably from the de Pima camp were laboring side-by-side with others obviously McAllister.

He saw neighbors of the Quitos', and Wyatt Slocum on opposite ends of a two-by-six. One of the deputies who had come to investigate the slashed tires incident was bracketing metal bars for scaffolds with the proprietor of the south-side shop where Miguel had purchased his new boots.

"You see?" Dallas whispered happily. "Everyone's working together. Nothing like this has ever happened before." She wrapped her arms around him again and hugged him energetically.

No one even noticed.

"It's a beginning," she continued. "Only a beginning—but then, how can a beginning ever be *only* a beginning, right? It's the beginning of the end of the feud, love. You've accomplished what you came here to do—everything's going to be all right now. You're going to be able to stay."

Through the activity around them, Miguel saw Father Kino heading their way. "C'mon, man," he shouted curtly, having shed his priestly demeanor along with his cassock. "We need every hand up on the roof."

Reluctantly Dallas released him. He turned to go, then turned back, a troubled look in his eyes. "But if coming together to save the Mission ends the feud, it has nothing to do with me. The people have done it all on their own. And surely God did not need me to bring the snow!"

As the logic of what he'd said sank in for both of them, Father Kino strode by, clapped Miguel on the shoulder, and steered him outside.

WHILE THE VOLUNTEERS inside worked to shore up the weakened ceiling, those outside shoveled the snowdrifts off the roof. Although night had fallen, the moon had risen higher, giving them enough light to work by.

Following Father Kino, Miguel mounted one of the ladders, then stationed himself at a section of roof that had not yet been shoveled. Soon he got into the rhythm of the task, found himself moving automatically—scrape, lift, twist, return; scrape, lift, twist, return.

It felt good to use his muscles, to feel them ache, to know that his body was still *real*. It felt good, too, to put his mind on hold so that he could stop counting the hours until midnight.

Finished with the section he had been clearing, Miguel found himself at the edge of the upper roof, directly above the west wing.

The west wing was the side chapel where a carved, corpselike wooden statue—some said of St. Francis, some said of Christ Himself—lay in an ornate, open casket. The old and desiccated statue, including bruises, blood and scourging wounds, was a favorite of the Indians. It was always covered with offerings—*milagros,* hospital bracelets, photographs, names written on scraps of paper and pinned to its clothing.

Miguel dropped his shovel down to the lower level, then used an attached length of rope to rappel after it.

There were only a few men on this particular roof. After a few minutes Miguel noticed that one of them was working his way in Miguel's direction, one shovelful of snow at a time.

Absorbed in his automatic rhythm—scrape, lift, twist, return—Miguel didn't notice the man again until the man had come up directly behind him.

Then he felt a small, cylindrical object pressed hard into his back, and he heard a hoarse whisper in his ear.

"Yeah, it's exactly what you think it is. Don't try anything funny or I'll blow you away right now."

There was the clink of metal as Miguel's wrists were jerked behind his back and handcuffed together. Then, prodding him with the gun still at his back, the stranger forced Miguel to the back of the adobe structure.

Just below was the lean-to covering what Mrs. Quito called her winter garden.

"Know anything about flying, de Pima?" the disembodied voice said into his ear, as the owner of the voice shoved Miguel off the roof into empty space.

The lean-to broke his fall. The man with the gun, taller and heavier, landed on top of him, and the lean-to, only a rickety wooden shed to begin with, collapsed under their combined weight. Together they plummeted to the ground and rolled, the stranger's arm locked viselike around Miguel's neck.

When they slammed to a stop against the garden shed, halfway between the Mission building and the old Indian graveyard, the man seized the handcuffs and jerked Miguel onto his belly on the ground. With bone-crushing force, he jammed his knee into the small of Miguel's back.

"We're takin' a little ride, de Pima," he snarled. "And just so's I don't have to shoot you before we get where we're goin'—" He whipped a dirty blue bandanna off his neck and tied it round Miguel's mouth.

MIGUEL HAD SEEN the short, round man before. Only once, and only briefly, and he wasn't sure where, but he *had* seen him.

Not that it mattered. The fat little man was giving the orders, but he was keeping his distance. It was the other two, his accomplices, that were Miguel's most immediate problem. They gripped his arms on either side with iron hands, despite the fact that *his* were still cuffed behind his back.

The red, flame-decorated high-rider that had brought him here on its huge tires was also familiar, and *that* he knew where he had seen last.

Not that that mattered, either, for Miguel knew he was not going to live to tell anyone about it.

God.

The God whose human birth was even now being celebrated all over the world; the gentle God of Father Sebastiani—doubtless the old priest had been disappointed, Miguel thought with gallows humor, when he finally met his maker—had come to collect His due.

The little fat man was nervous. As he hopped agitatedly from one expensively booted foot to the other, he berated the two thugs who now held Miguel immobilized between them. His voice quavered from tenor to a squeaky falsetto.

"Why is he conscious? You were supposed to knock him out! He's looking at me! Turn him around, don't let him look at me! I can't shoot a man when he's looking at me!"

One of the burly thugs looked uncertain. "You want him dead? That ain't the way I heard it. I heard you just wanted him roughed up good. That's all Spyder paid me for."

The little man wiped his clammy hands down the sides of his trousers. "I'll do it myself," he said, his voice cracking. "You guys want an arm and a leg for a cold kill. Where the hell is a person supposed to get that kind of money? Anyway, I can't let him go now, can I? Even if I wanted to. Not when he can identify me. Look at him, looking at me! I hate that, I just *hate* that!"

He turned his back to Miguel and the two who held him captive. Arms akimbo, he slouched on one hip and tapped his pointed toe impatiently on the ground.

Finally he turned around again. The coat of his pricey Western suit was pulled open across his ample belly, and despite the frigid night, Miguel saw wide circles of sweat under his arms.

He also saw a shoulder holster.

The man was a fool, Miguel thought. He was also scared; but a scared fool can shoot you just as dead as any icy-eyed professional. But for some inexplicable reason, Miguel suddenly felt strangely peaceful standing before this obviously troubled man. He actually felt . . . sorry for him.

"Okay, okay." The fat man spread his hands in front of him, palms down, as if keeping a lid on the whole situation. "Here's the way we'll do it. You hold him still and I'll—" Out of the holster beneath his jacket, he pulled a pearl-handled, chrome-plated Derringer 45.

"Uh-uh," protested one of Miguel's captors in no uncertain terms. "*No way*. You don't even know how to shoot that thing."

"That'd make me an accessory to murder," said the other. "Get yourself another boy."

The two released Miguel and slowly began backing away. Miguel slumped to his knees. In that instant a fourth man stepped out of the rocky wash behind them, and *he* was looking down the long barrel of an old varmint gun.

"Ever'one stay right where you are," said Rooster McAllister.

"DEVERS SLOCUM?"

"Yep, Devers Slocum."

"But, Pa, how did you know?"

Rooster hooked his thumbs into his suspenders and cleared his throat importantly.

"Well," he began, "I was comin' up to the Mission. I was late, 'cuz no one bothered to let me know what was happenin'. Guess they figgered there wadn't much a lame old fart could do. I had to wait till old Hoohah drove up to the ranch to fin out that the roof was cavin' in on the White Dove.

"Anyways, while I was heading up, I see Wyatt's high-rider come barrelin' down at me. 'What's Wyatt doin' headin' *away* from the Mission?' I asked myself.

"So when I got there and I seen Wyatt shoveling up on the roof, I yelled, 'Where's your truck, Wyatt?' He didn't know what I was yammerin' about, and right then and there I figgered somethin' was wrong. So I turned around and followed 'em."

"What made Wyatt decide to follow *you?*" Dallas asked.

"You crazy, girl? You think Wyatt's gonna let somebody get away with that truck? Not *that* truck! I do believe Wyatt *sleeps* with that beast! Anyways, he grabbed the priest's Subaru, Wyatt did. I heard him drivin' hell-bent for leather behind me, but o' course, I had a head start."

Suddenly Rooster's body sagged, and he eased himself down into one of the sheriff's chairs.

"What I'm wondering, Rooster," Sheriff Cobb asked jovially, "is how a fella who needs a cane to walk around his own house managed to make it through that wash?"

"Beats me," Rooster said.

Dallas turned baffled eyes toward the sheriff. "But...*why?* Why would Devers do this?"

"Wanted your job," Sheriff Cobb stated succinctly. "Didn't want to wait till the next election. Way he told it to me, figured he'd waste Mr. de Pima here. Hates de Pimas, anyway—you know how that goes. Didn't bother him any to kill one. Figured he'd cash in on the hate that divides the town.

"There'd be at least a token investigation, he figured. Figured you'd insist on it. And when it came to an investigation, figured you'd lose either way.

"If you allied with the southsiders—on account of you and Mr. de Pima being such, uh, good friends and all—the northsiders would turn on you. And if you allied with the northsiders, the southsiders woulda figured blood was thicker than water, even for a normally square shooter such as yourself. You'd've never won another election, even if you'd've lived long enough to see it."

Dallas looked at Miguel, slumped beside her on the hard wooden bench in the sheriff's office. His elbows were propped on his knees and his hands dangled loosely between them. Filthy, wearing shredded clothes, he looked about as weary as the very first night she'd seen him in the back of her courtroom.

"We'd like to go home now," she said.

"Sure, go on home," the sheriff said magnanimously. A good crime always stirred his blood. "Won't be needing you to make a statement until next week, seeing as it's Christmas and all.

"Merry Christmas," he added as an afterthought.

Once out on the sidewalk, Miguel turned to Rooster. "You saved my life, Mr.—"

"Call me Rooster," the old man replied gruffly. "And there's no thanks necessary. I figgered—mebbe I owed you." His gnarled hand fell heavily on Dallas's shoulder, giving it a little shake. "See you for dinner tomorra?"

Tomorrow.

"I'll see you tomorrow, Pa."

Rooster turned to Miguel. "You, too?" he asked.

Miguel hesitated. "If I can."

BY THE TIME Dallas and Miguel got back to her condo, it was past eleven o'clock. They fell together in a heap on the couch.

"Let me run you a nice hot bath," Dallas said. "It'll make you feel better. And I'll get a first-aid kit and doctor up all those cuts..."

"Later, *querida mia*." Miguel didn't move, except to slide one arm around Dallas's shoulder and the other around her waist. "For now, let me just hold you."

"How about some coffee?" she said. "Or a sandwich? We haven't had a thing to eat since breakfast."

Miguel shifted painfully, trying to find a more comfortable position for his bruised and battered body. Every inch of him hurt. A lot like it had when he'd first found himself here, he remembered. It seemed like a very long time ago.

"I do not need to eat," he said. "If I am going to stay, I will have the rest of my life to eat. If not, it will not matter one way or the other."

Dallas stood and began pacing back and forth on the red-and-blue patterned Navaho rug in front of the couch. "Miguel, I have something to tell you." She raked her fingers through her tangled hair, already drying in the thirsty desert air. There was a hesitancy in her voice, as if she weren't sure where to begin.

"I wanted to save this for a Christmas present... but then I thought, well, maybe if...if something happens... I mean, if something happens, maybe you should know now. It might make it...easier for you, if you knew."

She stopped pacing, and turned to face him, taking a deep breath. "I found out what happened to your son, Miguel. He lived to grow up. He came back to San Xavier while Father Sebastiani was still there. He lived a long time. And you have descendants, Miguel. One of your great-great-great-great-grandsons lives right now on the San Xavier reservation."

Miguel stared at her uncomprehendingly. "How do you know these things?"

"After you told me about Paio and your son, I did some research. I called Ms. Malone—remember her, the librarian at the Heard Museum? I gave her your name and Paio's—you didn't tell me her last name, but I figured out the year you must have been married, and then I figured, how many Miguel de Pimas and Paios could have been married in that one year?

"Father Kino was right. Father Sebastiani kept very complete records. Ms. Malone found the record of your marriage, and the record of your son's birth. Sebastian."

Miguel's eyes widened, as if he thought Dallas was performing some kind of magic.

She smiled gently. "It wasn't hard after that. Sebastian de Pima was not your average Papago name. The church's influence diminished about the time the reservations were created, but by then the county was keeping records. Luckily, most of your family stayed in this area."

Still sprawled on the couch where he'd collapsed upon entering the house, Miguel was motionless. He looked as though he had turned to stone.

"I—I thought you'd be happy," Dallas said, her voice uncertain. "Are you?"

Then she saw tears dropping slowly from the corners of his eyes. *"Querida mia,"* he said, "nothing in this world could have made me happier. To know that my son lived. To know that my blood went on in spite of all that happened to me, all that happened to my people...."

Finally he looked up at Dallas, tears still on his face. "Thank you, my little white dove," he whispered. "You are good. You are kind and good and beautiful, just as I knew you were." He reached out for her and she came to stand between his outspread knees.

Clasping her with his arms around her hips, he laid his cheek against her stomach. "If that is all I can take with me, it will be enough. That. And this."

He moved his hands upward, slipped the fleece-lined denim jacket from her shoulders, and let it fall to the floor.

"This day has not gone as I had planned," he said softly. "I wanted to love you all afternoon, until we were both so exhausted we slept right through midnight. I didn't want to have to say goodbye. But now I only want to look at you."

One by one, he began undoing the snaps of her plaid Western shirt, and when that was finished, he unhooked her bra and pushed its lace straps and the plaid shirt off her shoulders.

He had never seen her breasts except in the dark. He had never seen any woman's breasts except in the dark. Not Paio's. Certainly not Dorthea's. Why hide such lovely, tender flesh, especially from the man you loved?

If God had not meant them to be seen, he would not have made them so beautiful, so shaped for a man's hand, so magnetic of a man's eyes.

Miguel fit his hands around her pale breasts and plumped them in his hands. His fingers were as gentle as the breath as it came from his lips. "Sweet," he whispered. "Sweet."

Then he brought his hands lower and fitted them around her waist. He pressed her firm, flat belly to his lips. It would carry babies someday—whose? Miguel groaned, but he couldn't even be jealous, so grateful was he to have known her at all.

Dallas stood between his knees, her own legs melting bonelessly beneath her. Miguel felt her body slacken. He drew her into his lap and pressed her head gently against his shoulder.

"It is almost time," he murmured. It was his hope that she would sleep, and later, let him become a sweet but distant dream. He hoped her life would go on, and she would find love, as Dorthea had not.

Their eyes fixed on the red numbers of the clock radio in the kitchen.

11:55.

11:56.

11:57.

Dallas felt the blood pounding in her ears. She could hardly breathe. Miguel turned his face to press his lips against her forehead, not taking his eyes from the clock.

11:59.

Then together, three of the red numbers turned at the same time. *12:00.*

12:01.

With a tiny shriek, Dallas threw her arms around Miguel's neck. Warily, his eyes remained fixed on the red numbers, afraid it was a trick, afraid it was a mistake, afraid to believe.

12:02.

He expelled the breath he had been holding—not just holding, but desperately clinging to, trying to make it last as long as possible, for fear it was his last. His body sagged, deflated. And the next breath he drew was new air—the air of a new life, and a new love.

Dallas's arms were around his neck. He felt her warm tears against his skin. And suddenly he knew that his new life was going to be very different from the old because, for the first time in either life, without feeling ashamed, he wept.

TIME NO LONGER MATTERED. It could have been minutes or hours later when Miguel cupped Dallas's cheek and tilted her face up toward him. "Did you say something about a hot bath and some doctoring?"

Dallas sat up. "Yes," she said, smoothing away the tear tracks on her face. "You get undressed and I'll go run the water."

"Only if you will bathe with me."

"That could be arranged, I think."

After Dallas had vacated his lap, Miguel walked into the bedroom, shedding his clothes along the way. When he finally tugged the briefs down his legs and out from under his feet, he stood in the middle of the floor, trying to work up his courage.

He was afraid, but he had to know. It was the proof he needed. The last proof.

Turning slowly, he lifted his eyes to the full-length mirror on the door.

And saw, for the first time in one hundred years, his own body. Naked as the very first time it had been born into this world, it was dirty and bloody, with purple bruises already showing under the skin, but it was his, and just the way he remembered it!

In a cloud of steam, as naked as he, Dallas emerged from the bathroom. She walked up behind Miguel and slipped her arms under his. Standing on tiptoe to peek over his shoulder, she smiled at him in the mirror.

"Merry Christmas," she said.

Chapter Seventeen

"Dearly Beloved, we are gathered here today..."

In the Holy Land, the first Christmas morning must have dawned over a landscape very much the same as the one that dawned over the Tucson Valley this Christmas Day.

The rising sun first rimmed the distant cliffs in shades of purple, from the palest lilac and gentle violets, to the darkest amethyst in the shadowed crevices, then moved to the tops of palm trees, then poured itself across the bleached and arid desert floor.

The snow had stopped. The white drifts accumulated around the desert scrub glittered like diamonds in the morning sun. The poinsettia trees were miracles of another sort, sending their flamboyant red flowers straight up through layers of crystalline white.

After last night's storm, truly a miracle, Miguel thought.

He had been awake since dawn. He thought he might very well never sleep again, so determined was he not to waste a single moment of this new life that was his.

Just being alive to see this day was a miracle. A memory of Paio drifted into his mind, no longer sad, but fond, like the memory of a child he had known long ago.

Then he thought of the child, the boy, Sebastian. He had lived a long time, Dallas had said. Miguel tried to picture the boy grown up, a father, an old man, but his mind always went back to the solemn, serious child he had known.

He had had children, Dallas had said. There were descendants living today.

Miguel wondered if he might look them up someday. Not to tell them who he was, of course—who would believe it? But just to see them, to know that they existed, to experience the tenacious, unbroken root that led back to the boy, and to himself.

Dorthea. Fiery. Rebellious. Independent. He wished she could have been born in these times, when those traits were valued in a woman.

He remembered her mother nagging at her—*Don't go out in the sun without your bonnet or you'll freckle. Don't ride. Don't run.* And her father—*Don't go near that goddamn Indian scum.* He remembered watching her ride like the wind, her skirts bunched up under her knees. How she would have liked the freedoms that Dallas enjoyed—of wearing men's clothing, yet still looking every bit a woman, as Dallas did.

Nothing was ever lost, he thought now. Down through the generations, Paio was still alive; the boy was still alive. He himself was still alive, although where he fit into God's Divine Scheme, as Father Sebastiani used to call it, he had yet to discover. But he knew that, in time, it would unfold before him.

And Dorthea? She lived, too—in her own children and their children down through the generations, wherever they might be. And she lived in the woman who shared her nature and her name.

Dallas.

Miguel looked down at her, standing beside him at the window, wrapped in a white terry-cloth robe that swallowed her from neck to toes.

"A perfect day for a wedding," he said. "But we can wait, if you like. I know women enjoy planning these things—"

"No," she replied firmly. "We've already waited a hundred years—I think that's long enough." She laughed happily. "It's lucky we live in Arizona. There's no waiting period here—and I can issue us a marriage license!"

"BEFORE GOD and these witnesses..."

The church was full. Father Kino was gratified.

In addition to the regular parishioners of the White Dove of the Desert, there were also the townsfolk of Los Reales. Many of those who had worked through the night to rescue the Mission had returned in the daylight to see how their handiwork of the previous night had held up.

The magnificent murals in the vaulted ceilings appeared unharmed. Miraculously, not even the richly frescoed dome that soared over the church at its center showed any sign of cracks or water damage.

The old Mission, Father Kino thought gratefully, had been saved.

Nevertheless, he planned to keep the scaffolding and the wooden two-by-four supports in place for a while longer. Just as a reminder to the townsfolk of the night they had labored together on something bigger than themselves, and won.

Just in case they backslid, which human beings, he knew only too well, were wont to do.

"To JOIN *this man and this woman in the bonds of Holy Matrimony."*

Dallas wore a white dress, old but still beautiful, that she'd bought years ago for some occasion in Phoenix, which she'd long since forgotten.

It was a summer dress, but because this sunny Christmas Day had turned unseasonably warm, the sheer silk was entirely appropriate. Scooped-necked and short-sleeved, the dress was seamed princess-style, to fit closely to her narrow waist, then flare out in a full skirt that rustled gracefully as she walked.

At her neck and ears she wore pearls. Even their opaque iridescence took on a rosy glow so near to her bright, orange hair.

"WHO GIVETH this woman to this man?"

"I do," said Rooster McAllister.

His presence had surprised Dallas. When she had called him that morning to tell him of their plans, he had met the news with his usual chronic grumbling.

"Why you gotta do everythin' in such a rush?" he'd growled. "People'll think you're pregnant or somethin'. You ain't, are you? And who's gonna cook this damned scrawy-lookin' naked bird you got staked out in my fridge?"

Then, just before Father Kino had begun the ceremony, Rooster had rumbled up to the Mission in his old farm truck. He wore the black suit he saved for special occasions, almost exclusively funerals. Dallas had not seen it in years. His red hair was plastered to the sides of his head, and the few remaining hairs that were long enough were combed over his bald spot.

His red polka-dot tie, amateurishly tied, was wide enough to have been in and out of style a dozen times or more in his lifetime.

When he had stumped, panting with exertion, through the parking lot to the portal of the church where Dallas and Miguel stood, he'd groped in his pocket and produced a handkerchief, yellowed with age. There was a knot in one corner, and Rooster had fumbled to loosen it.

"This was your ma's," he'd told Dallas, when he'd finally gotten the knot untied. He'd placed in her palm a simple gold ring, with a single tiny diamond winking up from the center of the wide gold band.

"She left it when she took off. I allus thought I'd sell it, or hock it, but..." He'd shrugged, unwilling to admit his own motives, even to himself.

"Don't s'pose you even thought about a ring, didja? *Harrumph.* Didn't think so. You give this to him—" he'd jerked his head in Miguel's direction "—and let him put it on your finger when the preacher says it's time."

He'd swiped at his nose with the old handkerchief, then shoved it into his back pocket. "Your ma woulda liked that," he'd mumbled.

Dallas had handed the ring to Miguel, who'd taken it and put it in his pocket, then reached out to shake the old man's hand.

"If anyone knows any reason why these two should not be joined in Holy Matrimony, let him speak now or forever hold his peace...."

"Look, man, I'm real sorry about last night," Wyatt Slocum had said to Miguel right after Wyatt had climbed down from the Mission roof where he'd been inspecting snow damage.

"My brother, I don't figger he knew what he was doing. Devers, well, he's always been a little . . . highstrung. Not that it's any excuse, I ain't saying that. To tell you the truth, maybe we all been a little highstrung around here. Maybe for a long time. Maybe too long.

"But anyway, I want to apologize." Wyatt shuffled his booted feet awkwardly in the sand. "For Devers.

And for everything else I...well, anything else. Maybe we could just let what's past stay past, if that's okay with you, w'd'ye say?

"Say, Rooster tells me you probably don't know anyone in town to be your best man. If you got no one else in mind, I'd be pleased ..."

For the second time that day, for only the second time in both his lifetimes, Miguel found himself shaking a former enemy's hand.

"REPEAT AFTER ME: *With this ring, I thee wed....*"

Wyatt handed the ring to Miguel, and Miguel slipped it on Dallas's finger.

"*I NOW PRONOUNCE you husband and wife. You may kiss the bride.*"

Miguel smoothed Dallas's hair away from her face as if it were a veil. Looking deeply into her blue eyes, he saw the love, the joy, the till-death-do-us-part commitment that he knew she could read as well in his own eyes.

Dallas turned to face him. Slowly, reverently, as if they were the only two people in the world who had ever performed this ritual, he kissed her.

THE CHILDREN'S CHOIR, deprived by the snow of their Christmas Eve *Las Posadas* finalé, burst into song. They poured all the energy they had built up since December thirteenth into an unrehearsed but enthusiastic rendition of "Oh, Promise Me."

The green satin banner that proclaimed Gloria in Excelsis Deo, borne overhead by the two angels dressed in lace, seemed to sway in an unseen current of air that blew through the old Mission church. The painted adobe faces of the angels themselves seemed to smile.

From even higher overhead, from in the very peak of the frescoed dome, gray with the smoke of a million candles and filled with the breaths of a million prayers, Father Sebastiani must have looked down and smiled, too.

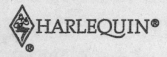 HARLEQUIN®

Weddings, Inc.

The proprietors of Weddings, Inc. hope you
have enjoyed visiting Eternity, Massachusetts.
And if you missed any of the exciting Weddings,
Inc. titles, here is your opportunity to complete
your collection:

Harlequin Superromance	#598	*Wedding Invitation* by Marisa Carroll	$3.50 U.S. ☐ $3.99 CAN. ☐
Harlequin Romance	#3319	*Expectations* by Shannon Waverly	$2.99 U.S. ☐ $3.50 CAN. ☐
Harlequin Temptation	#502	*Wedding Song* by Vicki Lewis Thompson	$2.99 U.S. ☐ $3.50 CAN. ☐
Harlequin American Romance	#549	*The Wedding Gamble* by Muriel Jensen	$3.50 U.S. ☐ $3.99 CAN. ☐
Harlequin Presents	#1692	*The Vengeful Groom* by Sara Wood	$2.99 U.S. ☐ $3.50 CAN. ☐
Harlequin Intrigue	#298	*Edge of Eternity* by Jasmine Cresswell	$2.99 U.S. ☐ $3.50 CAN. ☐
Harlequin Historical	#248	*Vows* by Margaret Moore	$3.99 U.S. ☐ $4.50 CAN. ☐

HARLEQUIN BOOKS...
NOT THE SAME OLD STORY

TOTAL AMOUNT	$
POSTAGE & HANDLING ($1.00 for one book, 50¢ for each additional)	$
APPLICABLE TAXES*	$ _____
TOTAL PAYABLE (check or money order—please do not send cash)	$ _____

To order, complete this form and send it, along with a check or money order for the
total above, payable to Harlequin Books, to: **In the U.S.:** 3010 Walden Avenue,
P.O. Box 9047, Buffalo, NY 14269-9047; **In Canada:** P.O. Box 613, Fort Erie, Ontario,
L2A 5X3.

Name: _____
Address: _____ City: _____
State/Prov.: _____ Zip/Postal Code: _____

New York residents remit applicable sales taxes.
Canadian residents remit applicable GST and provincial taxes.

WED-F

Take 4 bestselling love stories FREE

Plus get a FREE surprise gift!

HARLEQUIN

A M E R I C A N ◆ R O M A N C E®

He's at home in denim; she's bathed in diamonds...
Her tastes run to peanut butter; his to pâté...
They're bound to be together...

for Richer, for Poorer

We're delighted to bring you more of the kinds of stories you love
in FOR RICHER, FOR POORER—a miniseries in which lovers
are drawn together by passion but separated by price.

Don't miss any of the FOR RICHER, FOR POORER
books, coming to you in the months ahead—only from
American Romance!

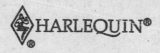

HARLEQUIN®

CHRISTMAS STALKINGS

All wrapped up in spine-tingling packages, here are three books guaranteed to chill your spine...and warm your hearts this holiday season!

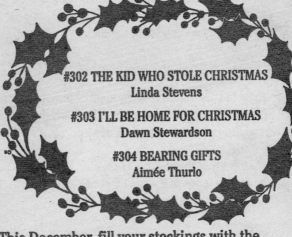

#302 THE KID WHO STOLE CHRISTMAS
Linda Stevens

#303 I'LL BE HOME FOR CHRISTMAS
Dawn Stewardson

#304 BEARING GIFTS
Aimée Thurlo

This December, fill your stockings with the "Christmas Stalkings"—for the best in romantic suspense. Only from

HARLEQUIN®

INTRIGUE®

HARLEQUIN
AMERICAN ROMANCE®

Four sexy hunks who vowed they'd never take "the vow" of marriage...

What happens to this Bachelor Club when, one by one, they find the right bachelorette?

Meet four of the most perfect men:

Steve: **THE MARRYING TYPE**
Judith Arnold
(October)

Tripp: **ONCE UPON A HONEYMOON**
Julie Kistler
(November)

Ukiah: **HE'S A REBEL**
Linda Randall Wisdom
(December)

Deke: **THE WORLD'S LAST BACHELOR**
Pamela Browning
(January)

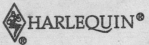

HARLEQUIN®

Don't miss these Harlequin favorites by some of our most distinguished authors!
And now you can receive a discount by ordering two or more titles!

HT#25483	BABYCAKES by Glenda Sanders	$2.99	☐
HT#25559	JUST ANOTHER PRETTY FACE by Candace Schuler	$2.99	☐
HP#11608	SUMMER STORMS by Emma Goldrick	$2.99	☐
HP#11632	THE SHINING OF LOVE by Emma Darcy	$2.99	☐
HR#03265	HERO ON THE LOOSE by Rebecca Winters	$2.89	☐
HR#03268	THE BAD PENNY by Susan Fox	$2.99	☐
HS#70532	TOUCH THE DAWN by Karen Young	$3.39	☐
HS#70576	ANGELS IN THE LIGHT by Margot Dalton	$3.50	☐
HI#22249	MUSIC OF THE MIST by Laura Pender	$2.99	☐
HI#22267	CUTTING EDGE by Caroline Burnes	$2.99	☐
HAR#16489	DADDY'S LITTLE DIVIDEND by Elda Minger	$3.50	☐
HAR#16525	CINDERMAN by Anne Stuart	$3.50	☐
HH#28801	PROVIDENCE by Miranda Jarrett	$3.99	☐
HH#28775	A WARRIOR'S QUEST by Margaret Moore	$3.99	☐

(limited quantities available on certain titles)

TOTAL AMOUNT	$
DEDUCT: 10% DISCOUNT FOR 2+ BOOKS	$
POSTAGE & HANDLING	$
($1.00 for one book, 50¢ for each additional)	
APPLICABLE TAXES*	$_____
TOTAL PAYABLE	$_____
(check or money order—please do not send cash)	

To order, complete this form and send it, along with a check or money order for the total above, payable to Harlequin Books, to: **In the U.S.:** 3010 Walden Avenue, P.O. Box 9047, Buffalo, NY 14269-9047; **In Canada:** P.O. Box 613, Fort Erie, Ontario, L2A 5X3.

Name: _____

Address:_____ City: _____

State/Prov.: _____ Zip/Postal Code: _____

*New York residents remit applicable sales taxes.
  Canadian residents remit applicable GST and provincial taxes.

HBACK-O